A CHRISTMAS CAROL II

THE RISE OF THE JUGGERNAUTS

By Nicholas Kaminsky

A Christmas Carol II: The Rise of the Juggernauts, by Nicholas Kaminsky

Based upon the characters created by Charles Dickens.

ISBN-13: 978-1-63587-186-9

For my brothers.

And for my sister too, I guess.

CONTENTS

CHAPTER 1

There were ten of them, each carefully chosen from among the best in the Order by the esteemed Master, each fiercely dedicated to the cause for which they now gladly risked their lives. Less intent men might have taken pride in being selected for so important a mission, but these men, hardened both in body and in heart by years spent toiling in cruel and unforgiving factories, were grimly focused on the task at hand. Dressed in simple workmen's clothes—for workmen they were, or at least had once been—they moved in silence across the frost-hardened ground as they made their way toward a single wooden door on the back side of the red-brick textile factory that now stood in the darkness before them, its shape outlined by the bright glow of the moon shining down from a cloudless, December sky.

Such a well-illuminated night was less than ideal for sabotage, but the Master had ordered that the plan proceed, and so it would. The men reached the door, quickly, but without rushing, moving in single file toward their target with all the confidence and determination of a column of ants marching toward a heap of sugar, spilled from a passing cart and forgotten on a London street by the larger pedestrians who go about their daily business, seemingly unaware of the tiny world beneath their feet. Like those ants, these men too seemed insignificant to the larger creatures with whom they shared, however unevenly, the world they all inhabited, those icons of industry and barons of business whose purses grew ever more bloated at the expense of their abused and neglected workers. But starting tonight, all of that would change. The Master had said as much, and this promise gave encouragement to the plotters now gathered at the factory door as they gingerly rubbed their scarred, cold-reddened hands together and breathed upon numbed fingers, doing what they could to maintain the dexterity needed for carrying out the destructive work that would soon commence.

Two of the more burly members of the company crouched down in the darkened frame of the door like two great gargoyles hiding from the ethereal, searching moonlight. With practiced efficiency, they removed large, double-bladed axes from the leather cases slung over their broad shoulders. Then, their hands choked up on the rough, wooden axe handles, they rose in the darkness and began to hack at the door in quick, powerful rhythm, first one, then the other, the sound reverberating loudly through the still night air. The door fell quickly, its hinges and locks unable to withstand the beating meted out upon it with all the efficiency characteristic of the cold machinery that hid in the pitch-black factory within.

The door had barely given way when a flash of light illuminated the dark interior of the building, and a thunderous crack ripped through the winter air. As if it were second nature to him, one of the axmen swung his weapon in through the doorway with tremendous force. There was a desperate, sickening gasp from within as the heavy blade cleaved into the chest of the hidden night watchman who had discharged his pistol in an attempt to stop the intruders. As the last echoes of his shot died away in the cavernous interior, the mortally wounded man dropped to his knees, the axe blade buried deep in his chest. His murderer—for all there gathered agreed it was murder, though they just as firmly agreed that murder was justified in pursuit of the cause—pushed heftily on the axe handle, knocking the watchman back onto the stone floor so that he could do nothing but stare, his eyes glossing over with shock, at the factory ceiling far, far off in the increasingly cloudy darkness above him. He was vaguely aware of the muffled crunching sound—or so it seemed muffled to his fading hearing—that accompanied the axe being pried from his chest, and by the time the flat edge of the blade came swinging down upon his bloodless face for the killing blow, he'd already faded out of consciousness and had passed into the sweet peace of death.

It was a pity that the watchman had had to die. Or at least it would have been, if there were a place for pity in the Order's mission. The watchman too, was a workman, a hapless employee to be manipulated and exploited by the perfidious bosses of industry until his use was at an end, at which time he would be cast out into the street like dung. Whether through old age, or injury, or some other unforeseen circumstance, his day would have come. The Order had merely hastened its arrival. In a way, they had even granted him an honor in allowing him to die in the fulfillment of the cause, regardless of the involuntary nature of his role.

The rest of the conspirators followed the first axman into the darkened factory, each stepping in turn over the fallen watchman, not a one of them showing the faintest sign of remorse or disgust or any other feeling in regard to the gruesome sight beneath their booted feet. Then, according to a plan rehearsed to perfection, they went about their nefarious task, each man keenly aware of the role he was expected to play in the rapidly unfolding drama at hand. The three lanterns they'd brought along for illumination were now placed at regular intervals upon the uneven stone floor, casting barely enough light to work by, yet just enough to create vague, eerily menacing shadows of the dark-framed machinery, the prime target of their malice.

With one man posted as sentry at the back door by which they had just entered, and another taking up position in the shadows by the still-intact main entrance near the front of the factory, the other members of the company went about their destructive work without the least sign of hesitation, four of them commencing an attack on the silent machinery with axes and mauls, the other four placing dynamite around critical points on the factory's walls and support columns. The separate destruction of the machinery was in all likelihood a symbolic gesture, as everything within the structure would soon be buried beneath an ignominious heap of rubble, but the Master had specifically ordered the dismantling of the machinery by hand, and so it would be done. The imposing silence that had hitherto prevailed now gave way to a cacophonous racket, amplified as the echoes travelled to and fro, reflected and deflected again and again on cold brick walls and on lifeless machines of various shapes and sizes.

The din of the machine breaking would have been enough to drown out most sounds, but what followed was not a sound like most. It began abruptly, issuing from a darkened corner at the front of the factory, and grew louder by the second. It was as though some strange contraption from another time or another world were coming to life, sounding strikingly like a powerful steam locomotive gathering speed as it lurches, then chugs, then races along its steel tracks. The men froze in their assorted places as their hair stood on end, their fanatical zeal momentarily cooled by the bizarre and terrifying event now taking place. A blood-curdling shriek issued from the sentry still hidden in the shadows near the front entrance, but was quickly cut off. The men peered into the foreboding darkness, their eyes scanning frantically for whatever horror loomed there. Their breath grew increasingly shallow and their heartbeats hammered as heavily, though much more quickly, than the tremendous footsteps now pounding along the cobblestone floor as the unseen menace drew nearer to them by the moment. And then, as they stared in sheer terror, a monstrous, metallic creature emerged from the darkness not twenty feet from them.

The creature, or contraption, or whatever it was, was like nothing any of the saboteurs had ever seen . . . or would ever see again. It stood erect, about nine feet tall, its tremendously wide, bulky, barrel-chested frame fashioned of heavy, blackened steel, the sections of which were held together with innumerable rivets covering it from head to toe. That is, if it could be said to have toes. It was supported by two squat, powerful-looking legs that shook somewhat crudely as it advanced, yet never failed to sustain the behemoth's tremendous weight as they propelled it forward step by certain step, all the while balancing it on a pair of four-toed feet, the "toes" of each reaching out in separate directions, each curved down slightly, seemingly clutching the ground as the creature lumbered along. The monstrosity's head, which was fixed directly to its broad shoulders without the benefit of any sort of neck, resembled a medieval crusader's great helm, though it was much thicker and lacked any sort of ventilation holes. What it did not lack was the narrow eye-slits of the great helm, though no mere mortal eyes peered out from these. Instead they glared, red-hot and intense, like the gaze of some primeval demon, as though an unquenchable fire burned within the belly of the beast. Indeed, even at fifteen feet, the now-trembling men could feel a dry, heavy heat radiating off the monster. But the heat, however uncomfortable, was not the chief source of their concerns; they were much more worried about what the two arms of the creature might mean for them. These were capped not with mechanical hands of any kind, but rather with simple, broad-tipped spears large enough to skewer an African rhinoceros.

The axman who had slain the watchman attacked first. He was a big fellow, hands hardened by years of labor in the mines, emotions tempered by months of training in the Order. He shook off the paralysis of fear, braced himself upon the cobblestones, and let out a fearsome cry as he charged the mechanical beast head on, raising his axe in a two-handed grip over his head as he prepared to deliver a crushing blow. He didn't stand a chance. As he closed with the dreadful automaton, it raised one of its powerful arms with frightening speed and accuracy and plunged its gigantic spear clear through the man's chest and out his back, the point emerging directly between his shoulder blades, impaling him and lifting him several feet off the ground with the force of the blow. The axe fell from his quivering hands, thunking crudely on the bloodied stone floor beneath his still-suspended, twitching corpse.

The remaining men stared, their eyes fixed in terror, their rigid bodies even more frozen in place, if it were possible, than they had been before the ill-fated assault. The seconds seemed to them an eternity as the equally motionless monster eyed them back, devoid of all feeling, those fiery eyes piercing the men's very souls. There was a grinding, whirring sound as unseen cogs moved within the beast, and two heavy steel doors slowly opened outward to reveal the inferno burning within its massive chest cavity. The men could do nothing but gaze in trepidation at that awful fire. Time stood still. Then, like glaze being haphazardly applied to a cake by a careless baker, a concentrated stream of molten metal began to gush forth out of the cavity. It targeted the men crudely, but effectively, searing their flesh, scorching them to death one at a time. Half were engulfed in liquid flame before the others gathered their wits enough to try seeking shelter, but it was of no use. The behemoth moved forward, stabbing with its spears, spraying forth the stream of fire, all the while staring lifelessly with its smoldering eyes. One of the men let out a piteous shriek that rose above the anguished cries of the rest as he bolted for the door. Another immediately turned and followed behind him, close enough to have been his shadow. Neither escaped the flame.

Within moments all of the saboteurs were laid low, some stabbed through with the spears, some crushed by the massive, four-pronged feet, all of them burned to varying degrees, all of them resting in a pool of cooling molten lead. As the agonized screams died away and the scalding liquid ceased its flow, one of the men, in an end-of-life moment of weakness the Order would have found shameful, unsteadily reached out a mangled hand and, struggling to extend his blackened arm, draped it across the back of his comrade who lay face down, charred and quite expired, in the pool next to him. His sorrowful gaze scanned the remains of the young man, the one he'd attempted to follow out the door an eternal moment earlier. "I'm so . . . so sorry," he quietly coughed out. "I'm so sorry, I . . . I'm sorry, Peter."

Small fires ignited by the molten lead burned in various places around the building, sending forth columns of ash and smoke, adding an additional layer of despair to the dismal scene. But by the time these fires reached the saboteurs' carefully packed bags of dynamite—with staggering but predictable results—no one cared, for the men who had carried them so confidently a mere half-hour earlier were all lying dead upon the floor of the now-deserted factory.

CHAPTER 2

The December morning air felt brisk, but Tim shrugged that off. Few things bothered him. And even if he were one to be easily perturbed—which he was not—he was at present too focused on his thoughts to care a button for the cold. His mind wandered to warm, vivid images of a past life, and a faint smile made its way up his right cheek as he recalled the joyful days of his youth.

He was alone in the churchyard this chilly midweek morning, gazing from the solitary hill at the serene, winding river below. As the first golden rays of the sun made their way through bare, frosted, birch branches to him, his ears caught the sound of a small flock of ducks drawing near. As he watched, delighted, several of them circled around in the grey dawn sky, swooped gracefully down, and landed on the partially frozen river, their feet skittering along on the ice, making a light, tinselly sound that was pleasant to the ear. Having landed, the ducks waddled across the ice and plopped one by one into the open water, flooding Tim's head with yet more memories.

He'd always loved coming to this place with his father to watch the ducks on the river after Sunday services. He'd never experienced more joy in his life than that which had filled his heart each time he stood there alongside the good man who'd worked so hard to raise their little family. Their Sunday outings—which always included church services and often a hearty discussion with the parson—had left an impression upon Tim that would last until the day he died. Those happy memories almost seemed to belong to another lifetime now. Still, as he stood there pondering, recollection followed recollection, each building upon the one that had come before.

Tim momentarily allowed himself to be immersed in the stream of these memories and permitted his mind to bask in the accompanying emotions. Soon though, he brought his thoughts back into focus and endeavored to organize his scattered, roving memories into a conscious narrative of his life up to this point. Such discipline was good for the mind; it was important to know where one had come from so that one might better see where he is going. With this purpose, Tim closed his eyes gently, relaxed the taut muscles hidden beneath his expensive garments, and took a deep breath of the chilly, winter air. Having shut out the cares of the exterior world, he sought to focus his thoughts. He began pressing his memories into a mold, summarizing them, making sense of them, organizing them into a chronological timeline of the meaningful events from his past thirty years. He pressed his eyes together a little more tightly, relaxed them again, exhaled softly, and reached back . . .

Despite all the disadvantages of his youth, his had been a happy childhood. As far back as his mind could grasp, the memories of time spent with his father were especially fond. He had been a sickly boy, it's true, and theirs' had certainly been a poor family, but they were poor only as far as material possessions were concerned. The love each member had held for all the others warmed their little home even when the meager amounts of coal for the fire failed to do so. And there had always been food upon their table—perhaps not in abundance, but at least they'd never gone hungry. This was especially true at Christmas time, that most glorious season of the year, when the peace and joy within their home seemed to increase, if it were possible, by tenfold. The spread that covered their table at that festive season of the year seemed to Tim's young eyes fit for a king. The goose, though always small, was always succulent, and the lack of raspberry dressing and other sides was made up for by their mother's delicious plum pudding, which she consistently worried would not turn out right, but which did in fact turn out just splendidly every year, much to the children's delight and perhaps even more so to their mother's relief.

In those early years, Tim had suffered from severe illness. As a child, he'd had great difficulty walking, and from a young age relied on a tiny, wooden crutch and iron leg braces to support his feeble frame. Even these unfortunate circumstances, however, had not diminished the joy of those formative times. In a way, Tim felt his weakness had even increased his family's love for him, and he recalled fondly that his father would often hoist him onto his own gangly shoulders and carry him through the crowded city streets at a delightfully rapid pace, all the while conversing, singing, and laughing, the two of them hopelessly lost in each other's company.

So long ago. That was all so long ago. So much had changed since those bygone days of his youth—some for the better, some . . . well, some changes had been more tragic. While always joyous, those early years had nevertheless been quite difficult, even verging on desperate at times. The strain of poverty had taken its toll on the Cratchit family as it had on so many other families in the city. But then the Cratchits' fortunes unexpectedly changed for the better. Tim's father's employer—a man commonly and quite justly considered a squeezing, wrenching, grasping, scraping, clutching, covetous, old sinner—had quite inexplicably undergone a dramatic change of heart and began providing for the Cratchits financially. This generous support allowed the older children to attend school, cultivate their minds, and make their ways in the world. Even more importantly, this most liberal benefaction had enabled Tim to receive proper medical care, which most likely had saved his life. For this, he was eternally grateful to his father's former employer, a Mr. Ebenezer Scrooge, who over the years that followed had become like a second father to him.

Despite countless hours of gossip and conjecture, Tim—or for that matter any member of the Cratchit family—never quite understood just what could have changed Mr. Scrooge so completely and so suddenly. While over the following years many a theory had been presented during the family's dinnertime speculations, none had proven entirely satisfactory. The explanation that was agreed upon as the most plausible was that Mr. Scrooge's nephew, a gentleman known affectionately by the Cratchit children as Uncle Fred, had finally prevailed upon the old man to change his ways. The fault with this theory was that it was well known throughout the entire city that Fred himself had been as shocked as anyone by his uncle's abrupt and utter transformation. To the present day though, Tim could not think of a more reasonable account for the whole mysterious affair. Nor could he fathom what had made Mr. Scrooge decide to leave his considerable fortune entirely to him, the youngest of the Cratchit children, when the dear old man eventually passed away in rather regrettable circumstances. Even after all these years, a part of Tim was still curious about what really might have transpired that Christmas season so long ago to bring about such a momentous change in his and his family's fortunes. Perhaps one day he would discover the whole truth of the matter, though at the moment that seemed doubtful and distant.

As he brought his mind back to the present, Tim again became conscious of the cold air nipping gently at his nose and other extremities. He opened his eyes, once again taking in the view of the winding river below. The ducks were gone now, and the time had come for him to be on his way as well. He turned to wish his father farewell. The plain, stone grave marker was covered in snow. He knelt down and carefully brushed it off with a suede-gloved palm. As he did so, the gentle rays of the morning sun fell upon the humble monument and began warming it, imperceptibly, but surely, even as they illuminated the neatly carved name upon its face: Robert Cratchit.

"Goodbye, father," Tim said quietly. He lingered a moment, raised himself slowly to his feet, and, his mental energies now recharged, turned to leave the peaceful, snow-whitened churchyard.

***

As he made his way across the grimy, congested city, dressed in his top hat and finest overcoat, a silver-pommeled cane in his hand, Tim's earlier recollections slipped into the recesses of his mind. He had business to attend to. Not the sort of business in which he specialized, to be sure, but business nevertheless. After nearly two miles covered at his typical, vigorous pace, he reached his destination. Stopping in the street to allow several other bustling pedestrians to move around him, he turned and looked up at the old counting house he'd inherited from his father, who in turn had been made a partner in the firm by Mr. Scrooge himself. A well-kept sign hanging above the door of the establishment read in gold lettering, "Scrooge and Cratchit." Though Mr. Scrooge had preceded Tim's father in death by several years, his father had not had the heart to change the familiar placard, having chosen instead to continue displaying both partners' names, in memory of his old friend.

As Tim opened the door, removed his hat, and entered the premises, he passed a row of judiciously busy secretaries. Seated on tall, wooden stools at even taller wooden desks, they were all hunched over their ledgers, diligently focused on their work, balancing books and performing other clerical functions of which Tim had no knowledge or care. As their youthful employer passed by, each one raised his head a bit and greeted him warmly—as Mr. Cratchit, of course. Tim returned their greetings with a smile and a slight nod of his head as he walked along the row of desks, his polished shoes falling with quick, confident steps upon the wooden floor as he made his way toward the back of the comfortably-warm building to speak briefly with his chief accountant.

There was no doubt that all of Tim's many employees felt a special sense of dedication toward him and revered him in an almost childlike way. His reputation as a kind, forgiving, charitable, pleasant man existed throughout the city. All of the many people who knew him would have, without any hesitation, described him in this way, and Tim preferred to maintain this appearance despite—or perhaps more so, because of—its questionable accuracy.

Tim's stop in the office was merely a formality. He knew perfectly well that his business was going just fine and would not have cared greatly if it weren't. The truth be told, he never really had a head for business of any kind. For this, in addition to more significant reasons, he left the daily running of the firm to his more-than-capable chief accountant and only dropped in from time to time to demonstrate that he was taking at least a cursory interest in the source of his large and growing fortune. After several assurances to the staff that he was satisfied all was in order, he made his way back to the door. Before exiting, he turned to address the row of bookkeepers in his customary, cheerful fashion.

"You men keep up the good work!" he said with a smile.

With that, Tim exited the premises, emerging once more into the robust morning air. His top hat once again resting in its proper place upon his sandy-haired head, he set off through the crammed and noisy London streets toward his second and much more important objective. Over the next forty minutes, as he moved further from the center of the city, the cacophonous crowds gradually grew thinner and their makeup slightly less respectable. Tim continued on, unperturbed. The streets narrowed and became markedly less well-kept. Still, he pressed on, all the while exhibiting a confident familiarity. Finally, after several miles, he found himself standing in a quiet street at his destination.

The structure before him was an old, ramshackle building in a rather neglected section of the city. A crumbling edifice of weathered, yellow stone, it had obviously not been cared for in many years. A terribly faded sign hanging loosely over the door gave the only indication as to what sort of business once occupied the dreary property. Tim could make out the first few letters on the dilapidated placard—F-E-Z-Z-I—but the rest were too faded to discern. He was not sure what had drawn him to this particular building, but he'd known from the moment he'd laid eyes upon it six months prior that it was right for him. Discreet and unassuming, it had thus far served his purposes perfectly.

Having glanced up and down the street to ensure the absence of prying eyes, Tim strode toward the derelict structure, mounted its crumbling steps, removed a large, brass key from his waistcoat pocket and inserted it into the badly tarnished keyhole. He could hear the tumblers clicking into place as he slowly turned his wrist. Then, with a firm push, he opened the heavy door inward, the sound of its aged, creaking hinges casting faint echoes throughout the interior of the building.

Tim entered quickly and closed the door behind him. For a moment he stood there motionless in the large, black space. The darkness was soothing, comforting to him, and he allowed himself a minute or two to rest there, secure in its cool embrace. The task at hand though would be more easily accomplished with a little illumination. He therefore reached into his coat pocket and removed a small box of wooden matches. Before long, the chamber glowed with scores of soft, flickering lights. Beneath and supporting each of these tiny, golden flames was a lamp or candle, which in turn rested upon a variety of shelves set at different heights and places throughout the large room.

Tim glanced about the still-chilly interior, surveying his personal dojo. Against the far wall, nearly forty feet opposite the door he'd just entered, stood a neatly lined row of wooden training dummies, most in various conditions of disrepair, a result of previous exercises. He made a mental note to scrounge up supplies for fixing their damaged appendages at some point in the near future. Along the stone wall to his right, his cherished weapons rack held a cornucopia of lethal weapons, including, but by no means limited to, a variety of swords, spears, *sais*, and *nunchuckas*—all of them important tools in Tim's shadowy trade. The opposite wall on the left-hand side of the room was covered in round, pine-wood targets, the bullseye of each shredded by hundreds of precise strikes from throwing spikes and *shruiken* stars. Tim again made a mental note, this time to remember that several of the targets were nearly chipped through to the hard wall behind and would need replacing before much longer. Even a primitive *dojo* required a surprising amount of upkeep. Finally, in the far left corner, two heavy, fabric throwing dummies sat slumped over each other like a pair of inebriates, just waiting there for their next round of grueling punishment. They were plenty dirty from being repeatedly slammed onto the wooden floor, but at least they didn't need any repairing.

Tim closed his eyes and relaxed as he took a deep breath of the cool, musty air. This place was home to him now. Not strictly speaking, of course. As far as the outside world was concerned, the respectable Mr. Timothy Cratchit lived in a somewhat pretentious granite mansion nearly a mile from here, though it was well known that he could seldom be found there, as he was often "about the city on business." But if it is true that home is where the heart is, then this shabby old warehouse was home to Tim. If he were perfectly honest with himself—and he always was—he knew that though he managed to put on a tolerably good show when interacting with others of his elite class at the numerous social events to which he often found himself invited, he always felt somewhat out of place in such glamorous settings. But not here. Here in the *dojo*, he felt . . . free.

After having made absolutely certain that the front door was securely locked, Tim walked quickly to the back of the room, his steps echoing ever so slightly as they fell upon the wooden floor. Reaching out a hand toward the far wall in the back right corner, he firmly pressed a very specific series of the rough, yellow stones, each of which depressed a quarter inch or so as he touched them. As he completed the sequence, a section of the wall half his height lurched forward several inches. He grasped the edge of it with both his hands and swung it slowly outward on hidden hinges to reveal the secret alcove behind. On the floor within rested a mid-sized cedar chest, its smooth surface lacking ornamentation of any kind. Above and behind the chest, hanging vertically from a pair of iron hooks on the wall, rested a fine *katana*, its flat-black pommel and scabbard as bare and simple as the cedar box beneath.

Tim crouched forward into the alcove and lifted the lid off the chest. A gentle smell of oriental incense and spices wafted out, to the significant gratification of his nostrils. Within a matter of minutes, he had stripped out of his fashionable businessman's suit and donned his coarse, white training *gi*, cinching it about his muscular waist with a simple cord. Thus appropriately garbed, he moved back into the main room and commenced with his daily training regimen, going through carefully honed martial motions that had long since become second nature to him.

Tim's well-toned muscles rippled with dynamic energy beneath his *gi* as he moved agilely about the room, diving, rolling, punching, kicking, sweeping. He was in great physical condition, yet this had not always been the case. For the first several years of his life, he'd been so sickly and weak that his parents feared that he, their beloved youngest child, might not survive, and perhaps he may not have had not their fortunes improved so suddenly with the conversion of

Mr. Scrooge. After this, everything had changed. Scrooge had paid for him to receive the best medical care available in England. This had been enough to save his life, and for that he was grateful, but he'd still been physically weak and remained reliant on that miserable wooden crutch for support. And so, after his twelfth birthday, his father and Mr. Scrooge had made the decision to send him to the Far East in order to study the martial arts, in hopes of strengthening his frail body. It had been a sorrowful parting, one which would have been worse a hundredfold if he'd known he would never see most of his family or friends again. But both his father and Mr. Scrooge had deemed it necessary, for his own good.

And so young Tim had set out by cattle ship on the harrowing journey around Africa and through the South China Sea. Having run aground in the fog on the coast of the mainland near Formosa, he made his way to the Henan province, where he was accepted into training at a local monastery and spent several years mastering the art of Kung Fu under the tutelage of the Shaolin monks. After four grueling years at the monastery, he departed on good terms and journeyed down through Korea, where he spent a short time honing his swordsmanship by training in the way of *Geom Beop* with a small group of Korean soldiers who'd deserted the army of the increasingly isolationist Joseon Dynasty and were living in hiding near the southeastern coast of the peninsula, disguised as simple fishermen. While Tim's skills with a blade developed rapidly during this time, his heart was ever more wistfully drawn to the islands across the sea, to that mysterious place called the Land of the Rising Sun. And so, with what little money he possessed—for he had left most of it behind in the Shaolin monastery as a donation in exchange for his training—he hired a genuine fisherman's boat to take him over the waters to the island nation.

Upon arriving in Japan, Tim initially made his way to the city of Edo, where he tried, to no avail, to convince a local samurai group to train him. As a reward for his dogged persistence, he'd been arrested and confined for several weeks with an elderly, plague-infested peasant, an experience he'd found most unpleasant. His fortune improved though when a prison caravan hauling him to a more remote location came under attack by a band of *shinobi* assassins who'd been hired to kill one of the Shogun's lieutenants and had mistakenly assumed their target was present in the caravan—as he should have been had not his lover's illness kept him back at the last moment. The *shinobi* had assassinated everyone in the caravan, guard and prisoner alike, in a vain attempt to ensure that they got their man. Tim's obviously European features were no doubt the only thing that had spared him from a similar fate. Or perhaps it had been his European features and his prowess with a sword—he had wriggled free from the overturned prison cart and joined with the *shinobi* in fighting the guards, skillfully decapitating three of the latter in the course of the quick but vicious battle. The *shinobi* had been rather impressed with him, and so it had not taken an overly excessive amount of cajoling to convince them to allow him to accompany them in hopes of proving his worthiness to join their elite brotherhood. Having agreed to his somewhat forward request, they brought him by a roundabout path back to their village fortress, hidden up in the mountains of the Iga province, and there, over the course of the next three years, they schooled him in the art of *ninjutsu*. It had been a radically different experience than studying Kung Fu. Very practical. Nothing flashy. Quite simply, Tim learned how to cleverly deceive his opponents and how to take their lives with brutal efficiency when the situation required it. And of course in an assassin's line of work, the situation required it significantly more often than not.

His formal training complete, Tim accompanied the band on numerous raids over the final year he spent with them. But though their targets were never innocent cherubs, working as a hired killer didn't sit well with his conscience and so, being greatly strengthened in both body and mind, he'd left the *shinobi* to at last return home to England.

Unfortunately, the journey home was more eventful than he'd anticipated. As his ship—a mid-sized passenger craft flying the French flag—neared the Horn of Africa, it came under attack by a vicious gang of pirates and Tim, knocked unconscious by the initial cannonade, had been taken captive. For three long, arduous years he was held prisoner, subjected to forced labor, cruel tortures, and generally inhuman conditions. But then, when his situation had seemed most hopeless, nature took pity upon him and allowed him to escape under cover of a violent spring storm. He'd delayed his departure just long enough to exact a brutal and gruesome revenge upon the worst of his former captors. It was a decision he regretted to the present day. He would never forget the sight of the half-dozen corpses strewn at his feet. Those men's gasps of terror and piteous, unheeded pleas for mercy still haunted his dreams. It was in that moment, while staring down at the lifeless bodies before him, that Tim finally realized he'd become little more than a ruthlessly efficient killing machine. Never again, he'd vowed. Never again would he take the life of his fellow man.

That vow against killing did not, however, apply to combat dummies, and Tim moved against several of them now in the candlelit *dojo*. He drove forward against them with amazing speed, shattering artificial appendages with a quick succession of both open and closed handed blows, sending showers of wooden splinters in all directions with each pass. He repeated the process, again and again, each time varying his movements in order to catch his oaken "opponents" off guard. When they had taken enough punishment, he paused for a moment to catch his breath and readjust the cincture about his waist. Despite the damp coldness of the room, the smell of sweat hung heavy in the air, and Tim twice wiped away the beads now forming on his brow. Then, without waiting another moment, he turned to begin practicing his assortment of lethal kicks and knee strikes against a heavy fabric training bag hanging from a chain in the corner.

After a short weapons practice, Tim spent some time resting upon the floor, regularizing his breathing and calming his rapidly beating heart. He then used a wet towel to clean his sweaty body before changing back into his businessman's attire. Finally, having extinguished the candles and lamps in the *dojo*, he headed back out into the street, carefully locking the large door behind him.

Feeling quite refreshed from his workout, Tim walked with a quick, self-assured pace down the street, making his way along twisting avenues toward the granite dwelling known throughout the city as the residence of Mr. Timothy Cratchit. Before long, he was in sight of the magnificent home which loomed there on the corner, rising above the street in all its glory. But something was clearly not right. Or perhaps it would be more accurate to say that something was clearly, terribly amiss. As Tim approached, he noticed a figure in the distance hurriedly making its way from the great house toward him. Though the man was not yet close enough for Tim to recognize his face, the tearful sobs were of an unmistakable origin. It was Eustace, the head cook.

As Tim approached the poor, weeping fellow, he was taken aback by the extent of the man's distress. His hands shaking, his face pale, his eyes reddened with tears, the trembling servant opened his mouth to speak, but choked on the words as he tried to form them. Now standing only an arm's distance from Tim, he closed his mouth and bit down forcefully on his quivering lower lip, trying in vain to regain his composure. After a moment or two of agonizing silence, he reopened his mouth slightly, cautiously, to make a second attempt. Tim felt a sickening knot twisting in his stomach as he instinctively realized the cause of the man's anguish even before he choked out those awful words.

"Mr. Cratchit! Oh, dear Mr. Cratchit, we have been searching everywhere for you! It's your brother Peter. He is dead! Oh Mr. Cratchit, he is dead!"

CHAPTER 3

The factory was a total loss. Richard Maximilian Wilkins shook his greyed head ever so slightly in a sign of otherwise well-contained frustration as he surveyed the dusty rubble heap of disintegrated red brick that had once been a highly efficient textile mill. This was by far the worst damage to date.

Several mangled bodies had already been extracted from the ruins. As Wilkins suspected, the corpses appeared to have once been members of this new anarchist workingman's association, the so-called Order of the Hammer. According to the reports being written up at that very moment by the police inspector near him, the whole affair had obviously been a suicide attack. These fanatics were getting more daring with each passing week, and everyone who knew anything had known it was only a matter of time before they would resort to such audacious tactics. So said the police report. Wilkins did not dispute it, and in fact even went so far as to encourage the young inspector in his findings. But inside, he knew the glorious truth. The Juggernaut guardian had done its job. Crudely, yes, but no doubt effectively. And perhaps the machines could be fine-tuned in the future, especially if certain rumors proved to be true. Wilkins smiled slightly, his aged face wrinkling at the corners of his mouth. All of the pieces were falling into place. As he started back toward his carriage, the impeccably-dressed old man turned his head to take one last look over the devastation. A pity, he thought. Though he was immensely pleased that the Juggernaut had performed more or less as expected, it still seemed a tragic waste of a perfectly good factory. He consoled himself with the assurance that very soon all of the destruction would be vindicated a thousand fold.

Displaying great nimbleness for his advanced age, Wilkins climbed back into his polished black carriage with all the assuredness of one who has the world at his fingertips. As the old man settled in on one of the burgundy leather seats, his driver cracked the whip, a sound that always brought a small degree of gladness to Wilkins' heart, even after so many thousands of times hearing it over the long years. Then, with a slight jerk and a jostle or two, they were headed back toward London. The Association members would want to hear a full report, and Wilkins was more than ready to give them one. Yes, he thought as he closed his eyes and rested his head against the padded back wall of the carriage interior, everything was proceeding according to his well-laid plan.

***

After an hour-long trip back to the city and a brief period alone in his austere personal chambers, during which he indulged in a bit of cherry snuff, Wilkins found himself addressing a gathering of his compatriots. He always prized every moment of this, though he usually managed to keep his satisfaction hidden from the others in the room. The feeling of being in control was . . . well, it was gratifying, like sipping a fine wine.

"The good news, gentlemen," Wilkins began, as he assumed his place at the front of the magnificent, dark-paneled room, "is that our steel guardian has successfully completed its first assignment."

The seven distinguished-looking men who were gathered about the round oak table before him visibly relaxed, a couple of them even breathing sighs of relief.

"The bad news," Wilkins went on, pausing ever so slightly for effect, "is that it is, shall we say, less than precise."

"In other words, your factory is a total loss," blurted out Mr. Newman, a young financier seated on the far side of the table who was as well known for his affinity for garish red suit coats as he was for his incredible—though mostly inherited—wealth.

Wilkins looked at the young dandy across the table. Not stared, not glared, just . . . looked. He looked at him in much the way a university professor might glance disdainfully at a pitifully stupid student. Newman knew better than to interrupt Wilkins, but the boy was one of those characters who often have great difficulty controlling their constant yammering, a fact which had gotten him into some trouble on several previous occasions.

The room fell awkwardly silent as the giants of industry and finance seated around the table held their breath like nervous schoolchildren waiting for one of their fellows to get a cuffing. After nearly half a minute—which all present would have agreed seemed more like half an hour—Wilkins mercifully glanced away and continued his presentation, having effectively put the young upstart back in his place without a word spoken. He almost allowed himself a slight grin, but managed to contain it. In their own places of business, these men were titans, feared and respected by their numerous underlings. But here at this table, they trembled before him as if he were a god. Everything was as it should be.

Mr. Newman slunk down into his seat, his face reddened almost to the point of matching his flamboyant jacket, though no one present could tell whether this was due to embarrassment or to anger at his utter humiliation. And truth be told, no one cared. All eyes were fixated on Wilkins, leaving the young banker to sink back into his place of relative insignificance.

Wilkins masterfully continued his presentation without missing another beat. The factory was, as Mr. Newman had so obtusely surmised, a total loss. Wilkins described the scene of the carnage very matter-of-factly and succinctly, leaving out many of the more lurid details. He maintained an even tone as he told the engrossed businessmen of the saboteurs crushed beneath the rubble and further informed them about the now-confirmed speculations that several of the criminals had been carrying explosives, which of course had been the direct cause of the factory's destruction.

There was a pause as Wilkins glanced from face to face. "The Juggernauts work superbly and are well worth the considerable amount of money we have invested in them," he declared. "But we do need to find a way to make them more . . . precise."

"And how do you propose we do that?" asked Mr. Riggins, a bullish foundry magnate seated next to Mr. Newman, completely dwarfing the younger man with his hulking presence. His tone was gruff and gravelly, yet full of respect.

This was precisely the window Wilkins had been waiting for. Now he did smile, a thin wisp of a smile spreading across his wrinkled face for all there present to behold. He turned his head and nodded to a servant standing silently in a darkened corner, who took his cue and carried over a square, pinewood box that he'd been holding throughout the presentation. He laid it upon the edge of the table and stepped back. As the servant retreated to his shadowy corner, the seated men gazed at the box, unsure of what to do.

"Open it," Wilkins commanded.

After some hesitation, Mr. Riggins reached forward with one of his tremendous hands and carefully removed the lid. The eyes of everyone seated at the table widened as the men leaned forward in one, fluid motion, as if under some mystical enchantment, to view the contents of the little crate. Inside, resting on a nest of straw, was a very large but otherwise quite plain-looking, round, iron doorknocker. Wilkins beamed as the men exhaled audibly in unison, each realizing the tremendous significance of the seemingly insignificant object that now lay there before them.

"Gentlemen," he finished in a rather satisfied tone, "I present to you, the Relic.

CHAPTER 4

Tim was stunned. His brother Peter, his only surviving family member . . . was dead. How could it be?

Eustace, the distraught servant who'd intercepted Tim in the street to give him the dreadful news, continued his story, explaining how police inspectors had found Peter's body amidst the rubble of a destroyed textile factory at dawn that same morning. Tim only partially heard the words the poor man was speaking. Peter, the elder brother he'd admired from his youth, was no more. A wave of grief and anger washed over him. Peter was—or now rather, had been—his last surviving friend or family member. While each parting had undoubtedly caused him some pain, this final one left him feeling like an empty husk, a hollow shell. In some ways, the grief now was even greater than when he'd learned by post of the deaths of his mother and two older sisters during a smallpox outbreak in the city. He'd been in Korea at the time, and so never had the chance to bid them farewell before they were cremated with the rest of the victims of the disease. It was a source of guilt for him even to the present day.

Yet, the pain now was even worse. He was more troubled at this latest news than he'd been when, upon returning to England from his Far Eastern adventures, he'd cradled his dying father's head as his body succumbed to the final stages of pneumonia, and the old man had, with his last, gasping words, told his son how proud he was of the man he'd become, knowing nothing of the atrocities his little boy had committed. Tim had not had the heart to disillusion him, though he regretted having to let his father depart this world believing a lie.

Yet, this current tragedy was worse. This was worse because Peter was the last person Tim genuinely cared about in the entire world, and now he was gone. Now there was no one.

Tim focused his attention back to Eustace for long enough to get the rest of the details about his brother's untimely end. Through the man's piteous blubbering, he learned of how Peter had been found burnt and crushed in a collapsed factory just outside the city, along with several other men. Perhaps even more tragically, it appeared that all of them were under suspicion of industrial sabotage. Not much more was known at this time.

"Thank you, Eustace," Tim whispered in a somber voice. The servant's glistening eyes met his for a couple of moments. Then the older man slowly turned and began to trudge back toward the great house, his mournful sobs resuming as he went. Tim decided to abandon his original purpose of returning to the mansion, which undoubtedly was filled with even more weeping staff. He needed room to clear his head. He needed to figure out what to do next. He needed to walk. Thus, as he set off to wander aimlessly through the city streets, he found himself, for the third time that day, dwelling on old memories.

Sabotage. How could his brother have been involved in sabotage? He still couldn't believe it. He knew of course that Peter had recently come on hard times, but how could such an upstanding young man have fallen so far? He'd once been such a promising youth too. Tim remembered how the whole Cratchit family had been so proud of Peter that Christmas day when he received his first job offer, an apprenticeship with Uncle Fred. Over the next several years, Peter worked most diligently for Fred, eventually rising to the level of partner in his firm. The two of them became close friends and prospered greatly together, but alas, it was not to last. Fred, always a noble and generous soul, had decided to go for a time to the Americas in order to involve himself with the growing abolition movement in the United States. Once there, he in short time established an anti-slavery printing press in the Kansas territory, much to the frustration of many of the locals who did not share his radical abolitionist views. In his last letter home to his wife, he wrote of the numerous death threats he'd recently received from border ruffians, but with the same pen he affirmed that nothing could divert him from pursuing the righteous cause he'd undertaken. The threats turned out not to be idle. Before the letter had even reached England, Fred was bludgeoned to death by a mob, his printing press destroyed, and his home burned to ashes. Two of Tim's siblings, the twins, had gone with Fred to North America and were, it was assumed, lost in the fire.

Upon Fred's tragic demise, Peter had inherited the whole of the firm. Unfortunately, it turned out that while his brother had a good head for accounting, he was not as proficient at managing an entire business on his own. Profits fell sharply and within two years he was forced to permanently close his doors, a fact for which his former employees held him no small grudge. With his poor fortunes, perhaps it was inevitable that he gradually slipped into heavy drinking and, as so often follows, fell into bad company, a development that undoubtedly caused their mother much anxiety as she lay afflicted with smallpox, breathing out her last.

Tim, upon his arrival home several months past, had done his best to reach out to his brother, but it was to no avail. Peter was too proud for help, too determined to forge his own destiny, even as it became ever more apparent that that destiny was one of only misfortune and hardship. Peter twice turned down Tim's entreaties, but even so, Tim felt some guilt for not having done more to prevent his brother's coming to such a deplorable end.

As he made his way up and down random streets, dodging in and out amongst the tumultuous crowds of carriages and pedestrians moving in all directions, Tim's sorrow gradually gave way to serious questions. Who were these saboteurs, and how had Peter fallen in with them? What were their objectives? And most importantly, how would he punish them for taking away his brother? All of these desperately needed answering, and he would find the answers. With this new sense of determination in mind, he turned abruptly in the street and began making his way toward the one place where he could best start his investigation and pick up the scent of those responsible for his brother's death—Scotland Yard.

***

The Order of the Hammer. That was the name given to Tim by one of the investigating detectives, an older police inspector named Bucket who had once been a friend of his father's. According to him, this secretive association of disgruntled workingmen was led by someone known only as "the Master" and had already perpetrated a number of smaller attacks over the last several months. However, the complete destruction of the textile factory was a new level of audacity for them. Not that they had been particularly docile before. They were, after all, militant anarchists fighting to bring down the country's economic system and with it the privileged few they believed it supported. Attempts to infiltrate the organization had been unsuccessful, to say the least. Two veteran detectives had lost their lives in separate incidents, the body of one found brazenly cast upon the front entrance of police headquarters. The Order of the Hammer, or simply the Order, as it was sometimes called, was not to be trifled with. So the police had warned Tim. Tim agreed. He would not trifle with the Order. He would mercilessly root it out and utterly destroy it.

Of course before he could accomplish this, he would have to find more information on his new adversaries. How many were there? Who were their leaders? From where did they operate? It was time for him to do some detective work of his own. Not as Mr. Timothy Cratchit, of course. No, this work would take him into less-than-pleasant areas of the city, places where his official appearance might raise some serious questions and perhaps unwholesome rumors. This was a mission better carried out under cover of shadow and darkness. Fortunately, shadow and darkness were Tim's natural allies.

By the time he finished his business at Scotland Yard, it was already late in the afternoon. His grumbling stomach reminded him that he'd not eaten all day. Though his training enabled him to go for extended periods of time without nourishment, he much preferred to eat regularly, when possible, in order to keep himself at full strength. He would need that strength tonight. And so he decided to drop in at the Pied Piper, a well-kept, working-class tavern not far from his counting house, for an ale and a bowl of hot, smoked-fish chowder.

As Tim sat at his usual table near the back of the establishment, his mind drifted again to the day's events, especially to the Order of the Hammer. Disgruntled workingmen, the police had said. There was certainly no shortage of them about London these days—or ever, really. He glanced about nonchalantly, eyeing up his fellow patrons. His adversaries could be anyone. Some of them might even be sitting in this very tavern with him. Nobody present at the moment looked particularly suspicious, but that didn't mean anything. Tim himself was more than capable of blending in perfectly with a crowd when he had reason to do so, and though he doubted very much whether anyone in this new, sinister organization had undergone so thorough a training as his own had been, he didn't want to totally discount it.

Having spooned down the last of his chowder and sipped the final drops of his ale, Tim made his way out of the tavern and into the crisp, evening air. The city was already quieting down for the night, at least in this part of town. With gloved hands tucked into his coat pockets and his cane propped under his left arm, he headed off on foot in the direction of the *dojo*.

By the time Tim once again entered his solitary fortress and pulled the heavy front door tightly shut behind him, darkness had fallen. He strode to the back of the room and once more pressed the familiar combination of stones in the far wall, swung open the hidden door, and crouched down beside the unadorned cedar chest. This time he removed and quickly donned his black combat *gi*, the unofficial uniform of the *shinobi*. During the time of his imprisonment in Africa, he'd believed the *gi* lost and was exceedingly gratified to find it in the possession of the guards when he made his escape. He was still further pleased to be able to reclaim it from their cold, dead hands. It had taken quite a bit of work to get the bloodstains out afterward—he certainly couldn't entrust that task to his housekeeper—but he'd managed just fine on his own, and it now looked as good as the day he'd eviscerated his first daimyo lord. The memory of the blood on his hands made him shudder a moment, but he reminded himself that now was not the time to dwell morbidly on past regrets. He had a job to do.

After adjusting the *gi* over his muscular frame, Tim pulled a pair of traditional, two-toed *tabi* boots over his feet and secured them by wrapping strips of black cloth numerous times about his calves. The soft fabric of the boots would allow him to move quietly about the city, in sharp contrast to the noisy footwear so popular with the several million other inhabitants thereof. The boots secure, he next wrapped the dark-grey sash of his *shinobi* brotherhood snuggly about his waist, securing the loose-fitting *gi*. Devoid of any sort of embroidery or decoration, the sash—which could easily double as a tool for garroting—was meant to be a perfect representation of the grim efficiency of the brotherhood: No flamboyancy, no high codes of honor, but rather only grit, deception, and ruthlessly achieved success.

Finally, Tim wrapped his head and face in the traditional black scarf of the *shinobi* warrior. Not only would this mask protect his identity, it would also help him remain concealed in the ever-shifting shadows by preventing light from reflecting off his face, allowing him to strike without warning and melt away without a trace.

Tim was now fully garbed for his mission. Only one thing remained—weaponry. He selected his usual favorites from among the tools of the trade: several *shruiken* throwing stars and knives, a half-dozen smoke bombs, a pouch of *metsubushi* blinding powder, and a pair of *shuko* climbing claws that were just as suitable for wreaking havoc on an opponent's face or body as they were for ascending the sides of towering structures. All of these he carefully packed into a small leather satchel, which he then slung over his shoulder and across his chest. Lastly, he retrieved his most prized weapon from its place of honor above the cedar box in the hidden alcove.

The perfectly balanced *katana* felt good in his hands. To most *shinobi* fighters, even the sword was merely a tool with which to deal out death as efficiently and impersonally as possible. They generally did not revere their weapons in the manner of the haughty samurai or European knights of old. Tim, however, was an exception. He'd opted for a *katana* over the traditional straight-bladed ninja-to sword of the *shinobi* because he preferred the former weapon's superior balance and overall better quality. In typical *shinobi* spirit though, he'd left the weapon completely undecorated, except for a small holly leaf emblazoned on the blade about two inches from the hilt. For Tim, this minor embellishment served a dual purpose. He felt firstly that the pleasant-looking but lethally-poisonous holly plant was a fitting representation of the double life he now found himself living, concealing his deadly warrior self under the guise of the good-natured Mr. Timothy Cratchit.

Perhaps more importantly though, the holly branch served as a reminder to him of the happy innocence and joy of his youth, especially of those ebullient days of many Christmases past. It was his hope that this reminder would someday hold him back from going too far, from again crossing the line and once more becoming—perhaps permanently—a simple instrument of destruction.

Tim slid the *katana* back into its black, fabric scabbard with barely a sound and mounted it upon his back with a pair of cords. Now he was ready. He walked across the room to the center portion of the back wall and stood between two of the wooden training dummies. There, so short as to be barely visible, a series of alternately placed pegs led twenty feet up the side of the wall to the ceiling. Within moments, Tim had gingerly ascended these and exited the building through a cleverly disguised trap door in the roof. Making his egress by this manner was necessary. It was much too risky to simply prance out the front door in his shadow warrior's attire, especially if anyone had chanced to see him enter earlier looking very much like the well-known Mr. Cratchit.

The night air felt cool to Tim as it brushed in the form of a slight breeze across the uncovered portion of his face. His warm breath escaped his lungs as a misty, white steam which his mask failed to conceal, even as the cotton fabric thereof quickly moistened and chilled from his respiration. He looked about him. The city was cold and lightly shrouded in a blanket of smoke and fog, yet it was aglow with flickering street lamps and the lights of little, pleasant homes beyond counting. Far in the distance, the Westminster Clock Tower stood erect, keeping its vigilant watch in the cold night sky. The sight of the city as a whole was rather pleasant to behold, but Tim had other obligations to fulfill this evening, and he doubted very much that these would lead him to any of the warm, cheerful abodes that now stretched out before him. No, his work tonight would require venturing to less savory parts of the city

CHAPTER 5

Richard Wilkins gazed upon the lovely young woman standing before him. She was petite, but by no means frail, having a well-toned build one might expect to find amongst an aboriginal people. Her skin was a shade or two darker than his, likely from the years she'd spent in the Caribbean. Her long black hair was pulled back behind her head and pinned up with a golden scorpion brooch that he'd given her as a gift some years back. Her facial features were pleasantly sharp and symmetrical, and her wide-set blue eyes sparkled as though an icy fire flickered behind them, revealing the passionate, indomitable spirit within her. Of all his many children, she, his youngest daughter, had always been his favorite.

"Is it true, father?" she asked.

"It is," Wilkins responded with a nod. "We have it, Annabelle. We've found the Relic. It won't be long before the next stage of our . . . operation, will commence."

She smiled at him, revealing the dimples on her cheeks that reminded him so much of her mother. Still, he could tell from the manner in which she tilted her head ever so slightly that she was not yet convinced of the wisdom of his plans. Hardly a surprise. While she was undoubtedly devoted to him, her strong, independent spirit made her question everything. This was not a trait to be discouraged. Indeed, it would serve her well when she eventually assumed his responsibilities.

"Let me tell you about," Wilkins began, but the girl cut him off.

"Father," she said, glancing down, "I have heard this story many times."

"So you have," he replied, unperturbed. "But I wish for you to hear it again."

She nodded slightly, her usual sign of deference to him. She was strong willed, but also obedient. Wilkins appreciated obedience.

"Let me tell you," he began again, "of how I first learned of the Relic." As if on cue, both of them sat down in their usual places on opposite sides of the enormous oaken desk in Wilkins' study. Wilkins poured himself a snifter of brandy and sipped from it as he spoke.

"The story, as you know, goes back many years, to when I first knew your mother. At that time I was working as a lowly apprentice in a textile warehouse. Your mother was a good friend of the owner's daughters, which is how I first made her acquaintance. I loved her from the moment I laid eyes upon her, but she did not immediately return my affections. There was . . . another."

"Ebenezer Scrooge," the girl interjected.

"Yes," Wilkins replied, untroubled by yet another of his daughter's interruptions. "Ebenezer Scrooge. He too, was an apprentice. I might even say he was my friend. Your mother, blinded by the emotions of youth, cared for Scrooge, and it brought her nothing but grief. He . . . rejected her. He broke her heart. Still, she pitied him until the end. 'Poor, poor Ebenezer,' she would often say. 'Poor, wretched man.' And she was right. Scrooge was wretched. And miserly. But even worse, he was weak."

Wilkins paused and looked across the table at his daughter. There was a moment of silence. She knew her part, but she was teasing him. She waited a second or two, then gave in, probably recognizing from the look on his face that he did not have the patience today to wait much longer. She'd of course learned such mind games from him, but she knew as well as he did that he did not appreciate having them used on himself.

"How was he weak, father?" she dutifully asked.

"He failed to see the larger picture," Wilkins continued, as he set the snifter upon the desk and leaned back in his chair. "He was too obsessed with mere money. He didn't recognize or strive to achieve the more important things in life . . . things like *power*. Money, as I have told you many times, can buy power, but only if you use it to do so. Scrooge did not. He didn't use it to buy anything. Instead, like the fool he was, he loved it for its own sake. And what good did it do him?"

"It drove him mad," the girl replied, this time without any delay.

"So we all thought," Wilkins said with a smile. "Everyone in London knows the story of Ebenezer Scrooge's overnight 'conversion.' From skinflint to saint, as the rabble on the streets put it. He fritted away all of his hoarded wealth, bestowing it upon those who'd neither earned it nor could do him any favors in return. And he made his clerk . . . his *clerk*, a partner in his firm. Madness. Wasn't it madness, Annabelle?"

"No, father."

"No indeed. Not madness, but *knowledge*, as I've come to realize now. Of course at that time I was as convinced as anyone that Scrooge had simply cracked. You should have seen the way he flitted about the streets, half-dressed and smiling like a lunatic, showering coin upon every beggar he happened upon. As he grew older, his condition worsened. His overly good humor remained, but he would ramble at times of . . . apparitions. It began gradually, with an occasional reference here or there to "the Spirits," but by the time a magistrate ordered him committed to the London Institute for the Insane, his hysterical outbursts and fits of giddy laughter had become regular occurrences.

"We all assumed, my colleagues and I, that Scrooge had simply tumbled down the final steps of his descent into madness. But something bothered me about the whole affair. What if there *were* truth in his ravings? After all, modern science has increasingly delved into the spiritual realm, allowing us to tap its powers. I myself have seen men healed of illness by the application of psychic energy. I've witnessed young women channeling spirits. Why, our own Juggernaut guardians are controlled by signals sent through the ether without the use of wires. If all of this can be supported by science, I thought, why could not Scrooge's tale perhaps be rooted in some fact? I finally decided to go pay him a visit in order to question him and get at the heart of the matter.

"It was a pitiful sight. There he was, my former fellow apprentice, wrapped in a restraint jacket, lying on a worn-out cot in the corner of his whitewashed cell. 'The spirits did it all in one night, the spirits did it all in one night,' he kept repeating. 'Of course they can, of course they can.'

"It was unsettling, but not frightening. He was . . . happy. While the rest of the Institute echoed with the moans and wails of the other unfortunate inmates, Scrooge's insipid joy could not be shaken. Hardly a moment passed that he did not have a ridiculous smile on his face. 'What did they do in one night?' I asked him. He glanced up at me, realizing for the first time that I was standing there over him, though I don't believe he recognized me. I repeated my question, and he told me the extraordinary story of the Spirits' visit, a story which you now know so well.

"As I left the asylum, I pondered what Scrooge had told me regarding that Christmas Eve so many years ago. His words played through my mind over and over again. I was especially intrigued by the alleged manifestation of his deceased partner, Jacob Marley. This spirit came, Scrooge told me, to warn him to amend his ways. When Scrooge saw him, Marley was transparent, and glowing, and able to walk right through closed doors. At first Scrooge himself had doubts about the reality of the vision, but the shade was very persuasive, and Scrooge was forced to admit the reality of what his senses conveyed to him. Even more significant for our purposes, he told me there were others like Marley. Many others. He saw them outside his bedroom window that same night, spirits beyond number, roaming the earth unseen amongst us. Such a terrific source of untapped energies, I thought. But how to access it? How to *control* it? And then it came to me: the door knocker. The door knocker was the key. It *had* to be. That's where Scrooge said he first saw Marley's ghost . . . or at least the face of Marley's ghost. That was the entry point . . . the portal . . . the medium, by which the spirit arrived in our world. If I could obtain that, I could perhaps create a bridge between us and the spiritual realm. I could tap the unlimited energies of the netherworld.

"Alas, the knocker proved difficult to come by. Scrooge's former lodgings had already been demolished, and all such objects sold off or scrapped. It took me five years . . . five *years* of searching, but at last we have found it."

The girl opened her mouth to speak again, but was cut off by the chiming of a clock resting on the fireplace mantle across the room.

"Well, my dear," Wilkins remarked as he looked down at his pocket watch, "It seems it is time for me to go. I do not want to keep the Association's members waiting too long, as we yet have some need of them. We will finish the story another time."

"Father," the girl said, leaning forward as he began to rise to his feet. "I *do* believe your story, but . . ."

"But you are still not convinced of the wisdom of my plans."

"I don't mean to doubt you, father. But even if this Relic has the power you believe it does, *how* will you harness it? *How* will you control it?" She paused a moment, then went on. "It seems to me that we already have sufficient means for securing our assets, thanks to your recent investments."

"I appreciate your concerns, Annabelle. You know I have always encouraged you to speak your mind, and I know that you have never shied away from doing so. But as I told the Association members, the Juggernaut guardians are effective, but terribly inefficient. It is my firm belief that the Relic will change that. Despite our best work, the contraptions are now quite crude. They are like large, walking furnaces. Yes, they can destroy our enemies, but they destroy everything else around them as well. You saw the reports from our textile factory. Imagine though, how infinitely more effective they will be when each is powered not by coal, but rather by an immortal spirit, snatched out of the ether and reincarnated in subservience to us."

The girl smiled again, but Wilkins knew she still had her doubts. All in good time, he thought. Once he successfully demonstrated his plan, she would believe him . . . as would everyone else. Until then, he would be content with her obedience.

"You know I have a great deal of confidence in you, don't you, Annabelle?"

"Yes, father."

"Of all your siblings, you have always been the strongest and the most fit to lead this enterprise after I am gone. I know you have your doubts about the course I am taking, but soon you will see that I am right, and ultimately you will inherit the tremendous power that I am about to unleash."

Wilkins spoke these last words as he robed himself in his black overcoat. Then, having gathered up his hat and cane, he made his way to the door of the study. Turning, he addressed her one last time.

"Be patient with me, daughter, for a few more days. Then you will see."

With that, he opened the door and left.

CHAPTER 6

This was it. Tim had burned through the better part of the last half hour scurrying over rooftops, leaping gaps between buildings, and slipping in and out of darkened alleyways. Now, as he came to a stop on the flat, worn rooftop of a four-story tenement building, he gazed about, reconnoitering. The night was a bit chillier than it had been when he'd started out, and while the city still stretched before him with its gentle luminance, the pleasantness he'd enjoyed earlier was entirely gone. A terrible reek wafted up to his nostrils from the filthy streets below, and grating cackles echoed out into the air from a broken window of the ramshackle dwelling upon which he was now perched. A most foul part of town. Good. He was in the right place.

Despite recent reform attempts, the St. Giles rookery was still one of the most notorious slums in London. But that didn't faze Tim. In many ways, he embraced the squalor about him. This was not the first time since his return to England that he'd visited a less-than-desirable part of the city. In places such as this, he was free to spend hours honing his skills under cover of night, melting in and out of the shadows like a wraith. The tightly-packed buildings and labyrinthine streets provided ample opportunity for him to sneak about, and the exceptionally high frequency of crime gave him more than a few opportunities to polish his fighting skills—non-lethal only, of course—against living opponents.

A sense of determination stirred within him as he climbed over the back edge of the tenement building, crouching low to minimize his profile, and gripped his hands about a rusted drainpipe in preparation for his descent. He *would* find those responsible for Peter's death. With great care, he lowered himself down the decaying, pitted pipe to a back alleyway. The winding street was paved with rough, uneven stone, and close on either side of it, crumbling brick tenement houses stretched up three or four stories, blocking out most of the light from the surrounding city. The walls were sparsely pocketed with windows, though many of these were dark or only faintly illuminated, as if by a single, flickering candle.

Tim had no complaints about the darkness; he liked it. He generally preferred to remain wrapped in the shadows, which was something quite easy to do here. Standing erect, his back pressed against one of the tenement's brick walls, he glanced up and down the narrow passage, searching for a suitable "informant." Approximately twenty feet to his left, at a point where the alley began to twist in a new direction, he noticed a stumbling, inebriated man making advances toward what appeared to be a couple of rather portly ladies of the night. Tim could not hear what the man was saying, but the women's giggles indicated that they found him amusing rather than threatening. The trio seemed quite oblivious to the presence of a shabbily-dressed individual lying on the frozen ground not two yards from them, quite still and possibly dead.

The inebriate might be able to provide some answers, Tim thought, but he decided it was more sensible to select his "volunteers" when they were alone. Turning away from the uncouth scene to his left, he scanned the portion of the alleyway on the right. This side was better illuminated, but also appeared to be deserted. Light streamed into the alley from a half-closed, swinging door on the side of the street opposite Tim. Judging from the cacophonous laughter coming from behind it, he surmised that this was an entrance to one of the neighborhood's countless gin-houses. Such a place would no doubt be teeming with the sort of men he wished to question. It was as good a location as any to begin his search. Of course it wouldn't be prudent for him to stride into the establishment garbed as a *shinobi* warrior. No, it would be better to let his targets come to him. He assessed the situation. A large mound of rubbish lying a few paces beyond the door would provide the ideal hiding place.

Having glanced about once more to ensure that no one was watching, he darted down the alleyway, making his way to the trash pile. Once there, he crouched down behind the heap of broken chairs, smashed bottles, vegetable peels, and other items he didn't want to even try to identify. Then, he waited. Eventually, someone would come through that door, and that individual would, with perhaps a little prodding, provide him with the information he needed.

"Eventually" ended up being much longer than Tim had initially hoped. He waited nearly an hour, hunched down in the sloppy, brown snow, his only companion a starving orange cat that curled up next to him for warmth. He did not drive the creature away for fear of causing a stir that might alert anyone exiting the gin-house to his presence.

All things considered, the situation was bearable. Tim had waited for targets far longer and in much less comfortable places than this during his time with the *shinobi*. There had, for instance, been the occasion that he'd spent two days in a septic pool, hoping for an opportunity to assassinate the heir of an aging warlord. His patience had paid off beautifully, but it took almost a week to remove the potent odor from his body and clothing, and no member of the *shinobi* band would come near him during all that time. Compared to that experience, and at least a dozen others like it, an hour in the snow seemed like a holiday. And now, it too was about to pay off. As Tim listened intently, he detected the sound of a growing commotion inside the gin-house. The tumultuous voices grew louder as they neared the door. He remained out of sight behind the rubbish heap, still as a portrait and poised like a leopard waiting for the opportune moment to strike.

The door swung outward, filling the alleyway with light from within the establishment.

"Get outta here, ya bum!" commanded a gruff voice, as a spindly man came tumbling into the alley. The man attempted to break his fall by reaching backwards with his twig-like arms but nevertheless struck his head on the uneven stone pavers and lay still.

Tim remained in concealment as the door closed, casting the alley back into darkness. A moment or two later, the voices inside died away, melding in with the general, raucous din. The outcast, still lying on his back where he'd fallen, began to stir. He probably didn't know it yet, but his night was about to get worse. Tim pounced from his hiding place, grabbed hold of the man's left ankle, and hastily dragged him across the frozen pavers, taking him further down the winding alley, away from any doors or windows. Then, crouching over the limp form, he scooped up a handful of wet, dirty snow and rubbed it into the man's face, hoping to bring him back to his senses.

The man coughed, and his eyelids flickered open. As his rolling eyes found Tim's masked face, he began to panic and tried wriggling away. Tim caught him by his left trouser leg and yanked him back.

"What can you tell me about the Order of the Hammer?" he demanded in a low, steely voice. The man stared up at him, his eyes wide with fear, but said nothing. Tim repeated the question.

"I dunno what yer talkin' 'bout," the man groaned. Tim glared at him a moment, then punched him in the ribs—not hard enough to cause any permanent damage, but certainly with enough force to make him think a bit more carefully about his next answer. "Tell me what I want to know," he demanded, his voice even and calm.

"I told ya, I dunno nothin'!" the man groaned back, as he tried to pull his elbows over his ribs to shield them.

"Wrong answer," Tim replied as he shoved his arms away and struck his ribcage again.

"I dunno! I dunno!" the man cried, curling up into a ball.

"Then who do you know who can tell me?" Tim demanded, pulling his fist back to his shoulder in an exaggerated fighting gesture, as if preparing to strike again.

"I told ya," whimpered the man, "I dunno nothin' 'bout it. I ain't ne'er even heard uh it."

Tim felt satisfied that the man was telling the truth. He rose to his feet, towering over the crumpled figure. The man groaned again and pressed his eyes tightly shut. Before he had the chance to reopen them, Tim slipped back into the darkness, leaving the man undoubtedly quite uncomfortable, but not seriously injured.

Tim was not discouraged by the first dead end he'd hit in his questioning. Or by the next. Or by the one after that. He spent the next several hours interrogating men he found exiting taverns or slinking in darkened backstreets. He questioned them all as vigorously as he had the first, yet none of them seemed to be able to tell him anything he didn't already know about the Order of the Hammer. The dawn was only a few hours away when he decided that he needed to change his tactics. And so he returned, via rooftop, to the place where he'd made his original descent down the drainpipe and into the first alleyway. The inebriate and his two plump ladies were no longer present, but the man who'd been lying near them hadn't moved a bit in all that time. Tim now crouched down next him and put his hand on the man's neck. His skin was cold and stiff. He was dead. A pity.

Tim grabbed hold of the deceased by his shirt collar and pulled him around a sharp curve in the alley. He then proceeded to undress the corpse, replacing his own *gi* with the man's outer garments. The clothes were threadbare, tattered, and a bit too small, and as Tim pulled the trousers over his legs, he found himself hoping that the man hadn't died of anything contagious. Having completed the apparel change, he stashed his own clothing, weapons, and equipment in a drain grate, keeping only a smoke bomb and the pouch of *metsubushi* blinding powder tucked in the pocket of his newly acquired, rumpled jacket. Finally, he finished his transformation by digging his right index finger between two of the bricks on the wall nearest him and smearing a bit of the slimy grime he found there around on his face. This wouldn't fool anyone who knew him well, but he doubted very much whether he'd stumble upon any of his regular, respectable acquaintances here.

His disguise complete, Tim walked back up the alley to the place where he'd interrogated the first individual hours earlier. The man was gone, but light still glowed around the edges of the gin-house's swinging door. Tim adjusted his ill-fitting garments as best he could, then reached out with his left hand and pushed the door inward to enter the establishment. As his eyes became accustomed to the light, he observed that the scene inside was just as rowdy as it had sounded from without. Workmen of every description congregated in small groups around tables set in every nook and corner. The hot, stagnant air was thick with varied tones of laughter and reeked of sweat and alcohol. Many of the men were engaged in playing card games, while others flirted with the dozen or so vivacious women who flitted about, delivering drinks amongst the writhing mob. At various places throughout the room, fights erupted, some in a spirit of anger, others, it appeared, in friendly competition.

Tim pushed his way through the crowd to the bar and ordered a tumbler of rum.

"You gotta way to pay for that?" the bartender grunted at him.

Tim laid down sixpence, and the bartender—a large, balding man who seemed to wear a perpetual grimace—served him without another word. Tim took a sip and waited as the golden liquid burned its way down the back of his throat. Satisfied, he turned about at the bar to further survey the room. The scene was indeed raucous, but while he did not for a moment doubt that it was common for men to be stabbed and bludgeoned here, he saw no immediate evidence of an organized plot rooted in this place. Who here though might be able to give him some more clues?

As Tim scanned the room, pondering, he noticed the presence of a boisterous man about five feet down the bar from him. That in itself was not significant, as everyone here shouted in order to make his own voice heard over everyone else's. But Tim noted that *this* man seemed to be inching his way along the bar toward him. At first he appeared to be stumbling about without a definite goal, but after a few moments of discreet observation, Tim felt convinced the man was quite deliberately moving in his direction. Sure enough, not three minutes later, he bumped into him, offering a slurred apology. Tim decided to play along and proposed to buy him a drink.

"Name's Arnold," the man belched, as he reached out and snatched an ale from the bartender's hand.

Tim laid another sixpence on the bar. He doubted very much whether the character standing before him was actually named Arnold, but that didn't matter at the moment. He was about Tim's height, though he had a much bulkier frame, which included a pair of massive forearms bulging out from his rolled-up shirt sleeves. The bright, curly orange hair on these was almost as thick as the matching beard that fully covered the bottom portion of his face. His eyes were a cloudy blue and his nose large and angular. His mouth was nearly hidden by the large mustache that grew down around it, blending into the beard, while a crudely tattooed squid reached its tentacles up the left side of his husky neck toward his clean shaven head.

Tim introduced himself—as John—and the two began chatting amiably, raising their voices so as to hear each other over the general din. As they talked, Tim's suspicions grew. This "Arnold" was not a good actor. Though the scent of cheap liquor was heavy on his breath, Tim could tell from his eye tracking that he was not genuinely inebriated. There had to be an ulterior motive for this conversation, but what was it?

Tim continued to play along with the ruse, planning his next move. When an opportune moment came, he would break off the conversation and directly confront his new acquaintance with a few pointed questions—questions he'd asked at least a dozen other times that night. He hoped to avoid getting physical in so public a place, but thought that if he caught the man off guard, perhaps something would slip out. And so he waited.

Finally, as Tim finished the last drops of his beverage and placed his empty tumbler on the bar, he thought he saw his chance and started to interject. At that same moment, his acquaintance abruptly stopped speaking and, without warning, leaned in toward him. He scowled and furrowed his brow so that the bright orange swabs of hair above his eyes nearly met in the center of his face. "What can you tell *me* about the Order of the Hammer?" he growled.

Tim's eyes caught the glint of the knife, and he instinctively reached down and intercepted the hand thrusting the blade toward his abdomen. He gave the wrist a sharp twist, releasing the weapon and sending it clattering to the wooden floor. The man who called himself Arnold glowered at him, but Tim didn't have time for a staring contest. He stepped in close and delivered a quick head-butt to his new friend's nose. As the man stumbled backwards, clutching his face, blood pouring through his fingers and down into his beard, Tim glanced about the room, his eyes scanning for additional threats. He'd been discovered and needed to make a quick exit. While most of the denizens appeared to hardly notice the scuffle at the bar, Tim counted five men who seemed a bit too interested. Three of them started moving in his direction. It was time to go.

Reaching into the pocket of his borrowed jacket, Tim removed the smoke bomb. As he stretched out with one hand to light the device's fuse from a lantern at the bar, he wrapped the other into a fist and struck "Arnold" in his solar plexus, just below his chest, causing him to double over, still grasping at his bleeding nose. With the bomb now lit and the fuse quickly burning down, Tim started pressing his way through the crowd toward the door. The three strangers were closing on him, and the other two now began moving in to cut off his escape. About ten feet from the door, Tim dropped the bomb. White smoke began pouring out of it as it rolled around, hissing on the floor.

"Fire!" someone shouted, and the gin-house erupted in panic. The sulfurous smoke spread quickly throughout the room, leaving patrons coughing and rubbing their stinging eyes. Throngs of them pushed toward the door, frantically trying to escape. Tim took advantage of the chaos to make his own exit, riding the wave of the mob out into the alleyway. Once there, he turned toward the door to see if any of mysterious men had been able to follow him. It seemed they had not. Smoke continued to waft out from the door as increasing numbers of patrons groped their way outside, joining their wheezing comrades in the street.

Satisfied that he hadn't been followed, Tim turned and dashed up the alley as quickly as he could. He needed his weaponry. As he rounded the corner and reached the drain grate where he'd hidden his equipment, he was disappointed though not quite surprised to discover that someone else had gotten there first. The two men looming in the narrow space in front of him had probably snatched up his gear shortly after he'd entered the gin-house. While they could have made off with it in that time, Tim guessed that they'd stayed in order to ensure he didn't escape. One of them now brandished his unsheathed *katana*, while the other prepared to hurl a throwing star from each hand.

Tim stood still, staring at the two men. Hiding his weapons in a too easily discovered place had been a mistake on his part. Attempting to use those weapons against him was a mistake on theirs.

After a moment's hesitation, the second man jerked his right hand forward, throwing one of the stars. His aim was off, and Tim easily sidestepped the projectile. As he did so, the first man let loose with his own attack. Shouting, he raised the *katana* over his head with both hands and charged Tim head-on.

Tim took a few, quick steps backward, feigning retreat. When the assailant was but a short distance from him, he braced his feet upon the ground and lunged forward, driving his shoulder into the man's waist and flipping him up and over his body so that he came crashing down behind him. The sword dropped from his hands as he sprawled out on the ground. Tim ducked low to evade another throwing star, which went whizzing over his head. As he raised himself, he leapt at the first attacker. The man tumbled backward, dropping the remaining stars, and Tim drove home the attack, showering him with a flurry of both open and close-handed blows. The man raised his arms and tried to block these, but Tim was too fast for him. As he pressed forward, forcing the man further up the alley, he glanced back over his shoulder. The second assailant had clambered to his feet and, having apparently forgotten about the *katana*, now charged again. Tim leaned his torso forward and shot his right leg back and upward, catching the man square in the gut with a side kick. He then reached up with his arms, wrapped his hands around the back of the first assailant's head, and yanked down, bringing the man's nose into devastating contact with his returning right knee. The assailant slumped to the ground, unconscious.

Tim turned back to the second attacker, who was doubled over, trying to catch his breath. He gave the man a shove, knocking him onto his back, then leaned down over him, grasped him with both hands, and pinned him to the ground.

"What can you tell me about the Order of the Hammer?" he demanded as he pressed his knee into the man's stomach.

The man's eyes defiantly met Tim's unblinking gaze, but he said nothing.

"Tell me," Tim demanded again. He raised his right hand in a fist over the man's face. The assailant stared up at him in silence for another moment or two. Then, he started to laugh. It was a low, throaty chuckle that emerged as he continued to gasp for breath. A wide, menacing grin spread across his face.

"You can't stop us," he whispered. "No one can."

"Stop you from what?" Tim demanded, pressing his knee a bit more firmly into the man's stomach as he leaned in closer. The man winced, but the smile remained.

"From fulfilling our destiny."

"And what is your destiny?" Tim asked him, easing the pressure from his knee so as to enable him to speak more freely.

"You can't stop us," the man repeated. "We will bring about the rise of a new order . . . a new order where the workman is supreme. Soon, the tyrants will fall. We will trample them under our feet. The Master has promised us, and it will be so."

"Enough rhetoric," Tim commanded, his voice icy and calm. "I want details. Who is this master? Who's in charge?"

"You can't stop us," the man repeated once more, his smile vanishing. Tim heard a popping sound and immediately felt an intense heat near his left knee. He leapt backward as a sizzling, white flame arched up from the right side of the assailant's torso, illuminating the entire alleyway. The man's laughter turned to howls as he thrashed about on the ground, the fire spreading over his entire body. Tim watched as he rolled across the pavers, through the various patches of snow, in what seemed to be an attempt to douse the flames. Then, before he could intervene, the man revealed his true intention. He rolled himself over on top of his unconscious companion, and within seconds both were engulfed by the fire.

Tim raised his arm to shield his face from the intensity of the flames. There was nothing else he could do now. The fire was too hot. He watched in dismay as both his witnesses blackened and shriveled before his eyes.

Another dead end.

Voices echoed from down the alleyway, undoubtedly from gin-house patrons drawn by the sound of the fighting and the glare of the fire. It was time to leave this place.

CHAPTER 7

The large, stone warehouse still smelled of gunpowder, despite the fact that it hadn't housed munitions since the beginning of the Crimean War. At that time, it had been damaged by an accidental explosion, resulting in the military declaring it "structurally unsound" and abandoning it. Largely forgotten, it sat vacant for many years, crumbling into disrepair down near the edge of the Thames, on the eastern outskirts of the city.

Yellowed government documents long neglected in the dusty files of some bureaucrat no doubt listed the moldering edifice as deserted, but this designation couldn't have been less accurate. Anyone who might have looked within the building's walls could have confirmed that it teemed with a level of activity not seen since its golden days as a munitions depot—that is, anyone who might have looked within its walls *and* been allowed to live. So far, no outsiders had managed to do both.

Fortunately for most of the very few passersby, the exterior of the structure did present the appearance of desertion, with all its doors and windows boarded tightly shut. The cracks between the concealing planks were so well sealed that none of the bright interior light made its way to the outside world. Instead, it remained trapped within, where it provided illumination for the nearly 200 men now assembled in a rectangular, military formation at the center of the cavernous room.

These men were soldiers, though they wore no uniforms. They had a mission, but it was not the cause of the state. Standing erect in the light of a dozen gas lamps, they drilled with rifles and bayonets, butting, blocking, and stabbing in unison. At the head of the body stood a stocky, muscular man about 30 years in age. Like all the others, he wore no uniform, but was rather dressed in the simple trousers, braces, and shirt of the average workman. Despite this, there could be no doubt that he held some position of authority, as the assembled men promptly obeyed his every shouted command, their respect for him in no way diminished by the sight of his crooked, purplish nose.

The drilling went on for some time, the only sounds the barked orders of the commander and the rhythmic stamps of the men's booted feet upon the wooden floor. Then, at the muscular man's orders, the others broke into groups of five or six and set about with individual combat drills, taking turns practicing their offensive tactics with daggers, mauls, and axes. The commander, hands clasped behind his back, walked amongst the little groups, silently observing their progress. The men trained hard—very hard—and more than a little blood was spilled upon the warehouse floor.

When all the men were thoroughly exhausted, the commander summoned them back to formation. Breathing heavily, their shirts soaked through with sweat, they stood at attention, waiting for him to address them.

"Brothers," the commander began, his fiery red beard and mustache highlighting his mouth as he spoke. "The Master is pleased with our progress and honors our sacrifices, as well as those of the comrades who have gone before us."

The men straightened their shoulders and stood up a little taller at the mention of the Master, a name they all held in the deepest reverence, though none of them had actually ever seen the reclusive leader of their Order.
His huge arms crossed in front of his chest, his feet spread in a wide stance, the commander turned his clean-shaven

head back and forth, surveying the assembled members as he spoke. The movement sent ripples through the tentacles of the sea creature tattooed in black ink upon his neck, making it appear to be almost alive.

"Brothers," he said again, his voice a little louder. "Tonight we will strike a blow against a new enemy—against a man who thinks he can oppose us, and who will now perish with the rest.

"My brothers!" he cried out once more, his voice booming in the sealed warehouse as he raised his fists up toward the ceiling. "The hour of our triumph is at hand. Soon, very soon, the tyrants will fall, just as the Master has promised us!"

CHAPTER 8

How could he have been so careless? That was the question Tim asked himself over and over as he walked down the street, heading east toward Newman's Court. The scene from the previous night played through his mind more than once, every time ending the same way—with him watching as his only two witnesses burned themselves alive before he had the chance to extract any meaningful information from them. How had he failed to see that second assailant's hand reaching for the incendiary device that must have been concealed within his jacket? This was not the first time he'd had a target resort to self-immolation. He should've been on guard against it. He'd gotten careless—perhaps even reckless—in his pursuit of those responsible for Peter's death.

The thought of his failure goaded him as he continued down the street, dressed once again in his finest, but certainly not feeling that way. His destination, the counting house, seemed an interminable distance in his mind, a situation not helped by his complete lack of a desire to go there. What he really wanted was for darkness to fall again so that he could continue his search for the elusive Order of the Hammer. He longed for a chance to correct his mistakes from the previous night. The members of the Order may have outwitted him once, but he would not let it happen again.

There was, however, an important question that needed answering before he caught up with the Master of the Order, whoever he was, and that was this: How exactly did he plan to punish the wretch? He certainly didn't intend to break his vow against killing, even for so foul a creature as this. The human body could, of course, endure an exceptional amount of pain, but the infliction of wanton suffering seemed to him to be a violation of at least the spirit of his vow. Still, the Master and his henchmen needed to suffer something for the destruction and death they had brought about. More importantly, they needed to be stopped before they could strike again.

The sudden, pleasant aroma of roasting goose momentarily pulled Tim's thoughts away from this dilemma. He'd been so focused on the issue of the Order that he hadn't realized his having already walked as far as the marketplace. Now, the tantalizing scent of a hundred different foods snapped his mind back to his present surroundings and he became cognizant of the high level of activity about him. While the marketplace along his route was always filled with numerous, bustling buyers heeding the cries of dozens of merchants, it appeared to him that an extraordinarily fervid spirit energized the place today. All about him, people beyond counting pressed their way in and out amongst the shops and booths of the various food vendors.

The sights and smells provided Tim a welcome distraction from his thoughts of vengeance. He stopped walking and stood there in the middle of the throng, gazing at the spectacle around him, soaking in all of its glory. Along the street, sellers at a dozen wooden fruit stands peddled such colorful morsels as plums and cherries and oranges and lemons. Great pyramids of onions and apples and pears reached up into the sky from every barrow, towering over the shoppers as they pushed their ways about, loading their baskets with figs, chestnuts, coffee, tea, and candied fruits. Above all of these carefully heaped delicacies, succulent bunches of grapes dangled from hooks set just high enough to ensure that their enticing contents would fall at eye level, seducing buyers with their juicy purple skins.

Tim's eyes shifted to the source of the wonderful smell that had first caught his attention. The poulterer's shop stood on the corner, a short distance from the fruit stalls. Here hung plucked birds of every size and breed, just waiting to be taken home and stuffed in the oven or roasted over a crackling fire. The poulterer's assistant could barely keep up with the crowds' demands for his employer's goods as he hustled about, fulfilling the endless, shouted requests of the merry horde. A similar atmosphere prevailed at the pork, fish, beef, and dairy establishments, where equally exasperated assistants struggled to meet the relentless demand for their employers' produce.

Tim had no need to purchase anything here today—his household staff saw to all of that sort of thing—but the whole scene reminded him of earlier, happier times, especially of . . . that was it. That was why the marketplace was so unusually active today. Tomorrow was Christmas Eve.

The thought of the impending holiday brought a smile to Tim's face. Even a shadow warrior could be allowed some joy at the blessed festival season. At the same time, his happiness was clouded by the realization that all of those friends and family members who'd played such important roles in past Christmas celebrations were now gone forever.

This gloomy idea turned his thoughts once more toward his deceased brother.

The *shinobi* had always stressed to Tim the absolute importance of not allowing one's emotions to cloud one's judgement, but here in this moment on the street, he could not help feeling extremely bitter at having been robbed of the last member of his family. The Order had to pay. The Master had to be made to suffer.

Perhaps he could make an exception to his vow, Tim thought. Just this once. What did he have to lose? His pledge to respect human life suddenly seemed much more fragile. Would there actually be any real consequences for breaking it—or rather, bending it? After all the people he'd slain over the last several years, would one more assassination really transform him forever into a hardened killer?

As these questions flowed through Tim's mind, he began to envision himself taking his revenge. He imagined the mysterious Master lying on the ground before him, pleading for mercy. He could almost feel the weight of his *katana* in his hands as he pictured himself raising the weapon over his shoulder and swinging it downward in a clean blow through the Master's neck, decapitating him. Blood gushed forth from the wound and oozed across the floor, seemingly crying out from the ground that Peter's death had been avenged. It mingled with other streams that poured forth from each of his past targets, who now lay before his mind, staring at him with lifeless eyes as the rivers running from their bodies coalesced, and the blood rose deeper and deeper.

Tim shook his head and the vision disappeared.

No, he couldn't do it. He couldn't kill again, not even once. If only for his own peace of mind, he would need to find some other way to punish the Order of the Hammer for its crimes. And find a way he would. As he resumed his walk up the street, he again became impatient for the coming of night. He desired more than anything else to be able to continue his hunt.

In short time, Tim had put the marketplace well behind him and had arrived at the counting house. While he currently had no desire to be at this place, his daily inspection round would at least provide a way to pass some of the daylight hours as he waited for the welcome return of darkness. He looked up at the sign hanging above the establishment's door. Scrooge and Cratchit, it read. Bob Cratchit.

The idea occurred to Tim that perhaps it would soon be time for him to follow more closely in his father's footsteps and pursue a respectable career—once he had carried out his vengeance upon the Order, of course. While he doubted that he could ever entirely make the transition from lethal warrior to man of business, the thought was at least vaguely entertaining.

Walking toward the old building, Tim noticed a small piece of paper nailed to the door just below eye level. At first he thought it might be some sort of advertisement left by an unscrupulous individual with little concern for damage to the property of others. As he drew nearer, he realized the note was rough around two of the edges, having been torn from a larger sheet of paper matching the color and texture of that used by his secretaries. Someone had scrawled an address upon it. The writing was crude but legible. As Tim reached out and removed the note, his hand rubbed across the text on the bottom left corner, smearing it. The ink was still wet . . . and dark red in color.

Tim let the paper fall to the ground as he gripped his cane with both hands. He pressed his thumb down on a button at the center of the pommel, unlocking the blade hidden within the shaft. Grasping the hilt tightly in his right hand while preparing to slide the scabbard off the blade with his left, he charged forward, plowing the door open with his shoulder, and leapt into the counting house.

A scene of devastation loomed before him, the likes of which he'd not witnessed since his time with the *shinobi*. Every one of the tall desks in the room lay knocked over, the legs of many of them broken off entirely. The same was true of the chairs. Hundreds of papers lay strewn about, ripped from the spines of mutilated ledgers. Many of the stray pages had themselves been torn to shreds, and everything was speckled with the dripping, black contents of violently overturned inkwells.

Amongst all the carnage lay the bodies of his slain employees, the right arm of each stretched out upon the floor, their hands pointing toward the center of the room where a quill pen rested at the edge of a large pool of blood.

Tim stood still, surveying the slaughter, realizing immediately the significance of it all. They knew. The Order of the Hammer knew who he was.

CHAPTER 9

Richard Wilkins stood alone in the vast steel foundry, inspecting the Juggernauts. The ten that the Association had produced to date were all lined in a row before him, silent and motionless. Their hulking, metallic frames towered over him, casting long shadows by the red light of the superhot furnaces which had given birth to them over the past several months. Unfortunately, the apples hadn't fallen far enough from the trees. Despite their improving technology, the Juggernauts did not yet differ all that greatly from the glowing furnaces whose light silhouetted them. Should the need suddenly arise to awaken the machines from their current cold, dark state, it would take several men at least half an hour to light and stoke the fires in their chest cavities to a point that they would have enough power to function properly. This was an unacceptable handicap.

The Juggernaut project had undeniably met with great success to this point, but as Wilkins looked over the machines now, he could see only their flaws and vulnerabilities. Granted, with their wireless technology, they were likely decades ahead of their time, yet they remained painfully crude and inadequate. Especially unforgivable were the external control boxes from which trained operators used a series of levers and switches to manipulate the Juggernauts' every action via signals sent through the ether. Despite the enormous fortune that the Association members had invested in the project, their scientists and engineers had as yet been unable to find a way to make the Juggernauts even partially independent of human control. They were tools—impressive tools, to be sure, but tools nevertheless. They were like mere hammers or shovels in that they could not function on their own, but rather required constant guidance. And wherever humans were involved, there was always the danger of incompetence . . . or treachery.

Wilkins sighed. Like cavemen, the Juggernauts were an admirable first step, but they were also just that—a first step. They needed to improve . . . to advance . . . to evolve. For this reason, it was imperative that he harness and use the power of the Relic. While science had helped develop the incredible steel bodies that stood before him, it had thus far proven unable to create souls for the Juggernauts. Attempts had been made, of course, but all had failed miserably, and the situation showed little sign of improving anytime soon. Wilkins was not one to give up easily though. If he could not find a way to produce new souls for the machines, he would reuse some of those nature had fashioned.

Once the Juggernauts were animated with spirits snatched from beyond the grave, they would no longer need those control boxes. They would no longer be mere puppets on strings, reliant on their fallible operators. Instead, they'd be bound only to Wilkins, the possessor of the Relic. With the awesome power of the fully animate Juggernauts behind him, there was little he could not achieve. Nobody would dare defy him. Everyone—the Order of the Hammer, the Association members, even the British government itself—would be forced to bow to his interests. The absolute power he'd sought for so many years would finally be in his grasp.

Only minor obstacles remained in his way now. Most significantly, he needed to reassure the Association members that his plan was both feasible and sensible. While they feared and respected him and would undoubtedly follow his lead in the end, several had raised concerns at the last meeting. Even Mr. Riggins, in whose foundry he now stood and who of all the members was most dedicated to him, had expressed some worry. Most of the questioning related to how control would be maintained over the Juggernauts once they were animated with spiritual energies. Was it wise to place lost souls in powerful new bodies? Could they be counted on to remain obedient? What would prevent them from running amok?

Wilkins could not tell the others that he planned to maintain sole possession of the Relic, and that, consequently, he alone would have command of the Juggernauts. They would worry that he meant to seize all the power for himself—which of course he did. He'd assuaged their doubts for the time with general encouragements and ambiguous statements, but, as with Annabelle, he could see that most of them were still not fully convinced of the wisdom of his plan. While he trusted that his daughter would never share her doubts with anyone but him—least of all with the Association members—it seemed that her opinion regarding the Juggernauts was a bit contagious. Several members had meekly stated that perhaps the machines *were* powerful enough in their current state, and that the use of the Relic might not be necessary.

This kind of thinking could not be permitted to spread, especially not so close to the approaching deadline. Wilkins' clairvoyant had made it clear that it was imperative for the procedure to take place on the anniversary of the original event. Tomorrow was Christmas Eve, the night upon which Scrooge had been visited by Marley and the other apparitions. If the Juggernauts were not ready for animation within the next day, they would have to wait another full year. This was not an option.

In light of all of this, Wilkins' most important task for the moment was to convince the Association members to trust his judgement. At the very least, he needed to ensure that Riggins remained committed to the plan, since the procedure would be taking place here in his foundry. Likewise, while her approval was presently of secondary importance, he hoped to demonstrate to Annabelle that he was taking the appropriate course of action. She would be the one who would someday inherit from him the awesome power of the Juggernauts, and it was imperative that she not reject it. She would need their strength to retain the loyalty of the Association members once he was gone. Due to her fairer sex and young age, they did not respect her as they did her father. Wilkins had strong suspicions that in the event of his death, at least one of them would attempt to usurp her authority in the Association. They would then gather about like vultures trying to filch the great wealth he'd spent half a lifetime accumulating.

He could not allow this dire scenario to happen. He'd worked too hard and sacrificed too much in order to make Annabelle his heir. She had not, after all, been first in line to succeed him. She'd once had five older brothers who, alas, were not as capable as she, but who nevertheless stood to gain the inheritance as long as they lived.

It was not without feeling that Wilkins had terminated his own sons, but this action had been necessary to ensure that his legacy would continue. The first had died in a carriage accident, riding home from a summer party on a dark, moonless night. Another perished while hunting, gored to death by a wild boar when his rifle misfired. Two were lost at sea, having gone down on the same ship while travelling to enjoy a holiday at the family's substantial property in the Caribbean. The last was murdered in his bedroom by a pair of burglars, who were quickly thereafter tried and hanged.

"Terrible misfortune strikes the Wilkins dynasty again," the newspapers had reported after the occurrence of each incident. Talk had even arisen in the city of a Wilkins family curse. Little did the gossipers realize that what seemed a series of tragedies had actually served to cement Wilkins' legacy by ensuring that his fortune would remain in capable hands.

Annabelle, since the time she could walk, had proven to be stronger and more adept than all of her brothers combined. From the age of ten, she'd taken a keen interest in managing her father's affairs, proving herself cool, calculating, and—when the situation required it—ruthless. At fifteen, she began playing a crucial role in the administration of his many enterprises. She'd taken over managing three separate textile mills, and had exponentially increased his fondness for her by nearly doubling their productivity in less than a year. At seventeen, she again earned his love by negotiating a secret contract smuggling weapons to the American Confederacy, a crucial deal that had allowed Wilkins' other businesses to weather the cotton shortage of the ensuing months. Shortly after her twentieth birthday, he'd sent her to the Caribbean where she'd spent two years proving her worth yet again by turning a failing sugar plantation into a veritable goldmine. She'd returned from that successful venture nearly a year ago and had spent the last several months at his side, learning from him how to properly govern an entire financial empire.

It was now time for her to learn more. Wilkins turned to face the girl, who had entered the room nearly two minutes ago and had been waiting patiently for him to acknowledge her presence.

"What is on your mind, my dear?" he asked her.

She looked past him and up at the Juggernauts, eying them one at a time, a studious expression on her face.

"They are impressive, father," she said at last.

"Yes," Wilkins agreed. "Yes, they are . . . but impressive is not enough. They must also be *effective*."

Wilkins did not for a moment doubt that a retort waited on the tip of his daughter's tongue, barely restrained behind her rows of flawless, white teeth, but she managed to maintain a disciplined silence. The Association members, led by Mr. Riggins, were now filing into the chamber and both Wilkins and Annabelle knew that it would not do at all for them to see *any* division between father and heir.

Wilkins surveyed the men. One was missing. "Where is Mr. Newman?" he asked.

"He's late," Riggins replied in his usual gruff voice. "No one has seen him since last evening."

"Very well," Wilkins responded after a moment of reflection. "We shall proceed without him."

Wilkins had never cared much for Newman anyway, a situation the young banker had not alleviated with his recent habit of ogling Annabelle every time he saw her. Despite the difference in opinion that they were currently experiencing regarding the Juggernauts, Wilkins and his daughter could at least agree that of all the Association's members, they liked and trusted Mr. Newman the least.

With the rest of the members now gathered around him in the shadows of the Juggernauts, Wilkins began his final exhortation on the merits of using the Relic to animate the machines.

"Gentlemen, we stand at a crossroads. It's been nearly seven years since we formed this Association for the mutual protection of our individual assets. Over this time, we have made great advances in improving our security measures. The Juggernaut program, to which we have all contributed vast sums of money, has proven to be very promising. *But* . . . it is not complete. Despite some opinions I have been hearing to the contrary, it is necessary for us to take one final step. The preparations are already being made. Tomorrow night we shall . . ."

Wilkins paused. His servant had entered the room and now stood staring at him from behind the Association members. Even in the reddish light of the foundry, Wilkins could see there was no color in the man's face. He nodded at him and the servant came forward through the gathering and leaned forward to whisper in his ear.

"It . . . it's Mr. Newman, sir. This morning two . . . two men delivered a crate to your office. We opened it."

"Go on," Wilkins commanded him.

The servant swallowed hard. "Inside were his . . . his remains, sir."

With trembling hands, the servant removed a bloodstained piece of paper from his pocket and handed it to Wilkins, who carefully unfolded it.

"Do we know the location of this address?" Wilkins asked the servant in a low voice.

"It's down . . . down near the river," the man stammered.

Wilkins looked back at the note.

"What is this?" he asked, gesturing to a hole at its center.

"That's how we found the message, sir. It was . . . it was stuck to Mr. Newman's chest. With a knife."

Nodding, Wilkins dismissed the servant, who hurried from the room as quickly as possible. He then turned back to face the Association members and Annabelle. They were all staring at him in bewilderment.

"Mr. Newman is dead," he announced. "Dead and thoroughly dismembered."

"What? How?" asked Mr. Riggins.

"It seems," explained Wilkins, his voice even and calm, "that this Order of the Hammer has somehow discovered who we are."

"Then we are all in danger!" interjected Mr. Niles, a banker who was not particularly known for his calmness under pressure. All of the others, with the exception of Mr. Riggins, echoed his opinion.

"What is written in that note?" asked Mr. Riggins. Wilkins handed over the paper and the men passed it about, studying the address, being careful not to get the blood on their hands.

"We need to send out the Juggernauts to deal with this at once," Mr. Niles wailed.

"We haven't much time," bemoaned another member, as the hysteria began to grow.

"Gentlemen, I think we are getting ahead of ourselves," Wilkins admonished them. "Why would these madmen provide us with their location unless they were setting a trap for us? Let us wait to strike until after tomorrow night. Once the procedure is completed, the Juggernauts will be *invincible*. We will then be able to crush our enemies with one unstoppable blow."

"We may not have until tomorrow night!" Mr. Niles shot back. "We cannot sit here waiting to be murdered while *you* dabble in your soothsaying and black magic!"

Wilkins furrowed his brow and gave Mr. Niles a cold look, but it was of no use. The members' fear for their lives currently outweighed their dread of him. He was losing control. The time had come to bargain.

"Very well," he said. "Perhaps we might . . . compromise."

"What do you propose?" asked Mr. Niles, his voice somewhat less agitated. The rest of the men fell silent, their eyes fixated on Wilkins as they waited to hear the new strategy.

"Tonight," explained Wilkins, "We will send the Juggernauts to strike at the Order of the Hammer.

Tomorrow night, we *will* go forward with the procedure, using the Relic to animate the Juggernauts. There will be no backtracking, no questioning, no doubting. Are we in agreement?"

Murmurs of "Yes, yes" came from the men as they nodded their heads.

"Yes," added Mr. Riggins. "We should strike while the iron is hot."

Wilkins glanced over at Annabelle, who was standing off to his left, a few feet behind the congregated Association members. Throughout the proceedings, she had remained collected and silent, as he expected of her. Now, she gave him a slight smile which did not quite convey approval.

Wilkins looked back toward the Association members, most of whom were still babbling their stamps of approval for the imminent assault. One by one, they stopped speaking as they noticed him observing them. Within moments, the room had grown silent. Wilkins was in control once more. Everyone waited for his final words.

"Mr. Riggins, assemble your men. The Juggernauts attack tonight."

CHAPTER 10

Despite his use of *shinobi* techniques for walking silently, the freshly fallen snow crunched under Tim's feet as he carefully stepped his way along the embankment of the frozen river. Ten paces back, his tracks had already vanished, filled in with quickly accumulating, soft white powder. A strong wind whipped at his *gi*, pressing it tightly against the front of his body while causing the looser portions to flap violently behind him. He was thankful for the presence of his mask, as the small areas of exposed skin on his upper face and hands were beginning to go numb, an early indicator of frostbite. Visibility was poor, a situation not at all helped by the constant stream of icy snowflakes blowing into his eyes. He hugged the shoreline, groping his way eastward along the course of the river. Eventually it would lead him right to his destination.

While it would have been much easier to walk along the city streets to the front door of his objective this evening, Tim was not so foolish as to march head-on into such an obvious a trap. As the corpses of his employees could attest, the Order of the Hammer had gone to extreme lengths in order to lure him to this place tonight. He doubted very much that their intention was to invite him over for tea. Chances were high that, even with the precautions he was taking, he would find himself in considerable trouble before the night was over. But, if the Order wanted trouble, he would not shrink from bringing it to them.

He thought back to the gruesome scene at the counting house. To say that he had not been troubled by the sight of his slain employees would be untrue, but he now felt a certain calmness of spirit in knowing without question that he was treading the only path available to him. The minor temptation he'd experienced earlier to forgo the life of a warrior had dissipated with the last, pained breaths of his secretaries.

After making the grisly discovery that afternoon, he had contacted Scotland Yard to report the murders. The main office had sent detectives, and the investigation was currently underway. Early indicators pointed to what he already knew—that the Order of the Hammer had struck again. Though he appreciated their quick assistance, he had decided not to tell the detectives about the note listing the address toward which he was now heading. Cataloging bodies and alerting next of kin was an appropriate job for the police. Exacting retribution—well, that was something he intended to take care of on his own.

For his sake much more than that of his enemies, Tim was still determined not to claim any lives. The human body, though, could endure an incredible amount of pain without succumbing to it, and he intended to inflict plenty of that tonight. While he had some lingering concerns about taking his crusade too far, he was determined to stop or at least cripple the Order of the Hammer. Peter—and now his employees—needed to be avenged. Even more importantly, the Order needed to be stamped out before anyone else got killed. Though it might cost him his own life, he was determined to accomplish both of these ends tonight.

He stopped walking, taking momentary shelter behind a large, fallen tree, and removed a map from his pocket. A small, black circle marked his goal. It was not much further. Good. Very soon he would be out of this blizzard . . . and into the frying pan.

Pocketing the map, he continued on through the winter storm. In short time, the blurry outlines of large warehouse buildings began appearing along the shoreline.

Their dark forms were barely visible in the blowing snow, but beneath many of them, drainage pipes jutted out from the embankment, reaching toward the river's edge. Though much had been done since Tim's youth to improve the city's sewer systems and clean up the Thames, plenty of drainage still flowed into the waterway, especially from older buildings like these.

After twenty minutes, Tim stopped to check his map once more. It appeared that the warehouse in front of him now matched up with the location of the address the Order had so dramatically left on the counting house door. Just as he'd hoped, a large drainage pipe ran out to the river fifteen feet below the base of the building. Measuring about two feet in diameter, it would be just large enough for him to crawl through.

Having removed his *katana* from his back and tucked it into the sash about his waist, Tim squeezed into the pipe. The metal was extremely cold, and his exposed fingers kept sticking to it as he crawled further inside. Still, it was a relief to finally be out of the wind and snow.

The narrow space gave him barely enough room to reach his arms, one at a time, in front of his head, allowing him to pull himself forward through the tube toward the faint light glimmering at the far end, probably thirty feet away. Adapting to such claustrophobic conditions had been one of the most challenging aspects of his *shinobi* training, yet he'd conquered those fears long ago, and they seemed almost childish to him now.

The pipe grew a few degrees warmer as it entered the embankment and stretched underground. Pulling with his fingers, pushing with his toes, and rocking back and forth with his shoulders and hips, Tim wriggled his way toward the light. Though he was getting closer to the other end, he heard no sounds to indicate human activity ahead. Most likely the Order members were lying in wait to ambush him. They probably expected him to come by a more traditional route—a door, a window, or maybe even a chimney—but if they had any intelligence at all, they'd also be keeping an eye on the sewer drain. Despite his precautions, he was most certainly heading into a trap. It was one he looked forward to springing.

Now at the end of the tunnel, Tim cautiously poked his head forward into a small, subterranean chamber and craned his neck to glance upward. Bright light shone down from a grate about ten feet above, but there were still no sounds of any activity. They were waiting for him.

Being careful to remain as silent as possible, Tim gripped the outside edges of the tunnel with both hands and pulled himself forward into the chamber. The walls were squared, about four feet by four feet, and made of crude stone held together with crumbling mortar. It would be an easy climb. With his *katana* mounted once more on his back, he spread his arms and legs, pressing his feet and palms firmly against the sides of the chamber. He took several deep breaths, inhaling through his nose, exhaling through his mouth. He needed to ensure that his muscles had plenty of oxygen for the task ahead. Then, looking up once more, he began his ascent.

At the top of the chamber, Tim peered through the iron floor grate, its surface thick with decades of orange rust. The large room above was well lit but appeared to be deserted, at least within his limited field of vision. Still no sound of human activity either. They were up there though. They had to be. The only question was, how many of them were there? There was one way to find out.

Pressing his calves firmly against the sides of the chamber to hold himself up with his legs, Tim reached back into his pouch and drew out several smoke bombs and a small box of matches. This would need to be done quickly. Using both hands, he lit the bombs. Then, with their fuses rapidly burning down, he dropped the expired match and pushed up on the grate with his right hand, forcing it open a couple of inches. He set the devices along the edge of the warehouse floor and began flicking them out with his left index finger, sending them rolling in all directions, hissing and spewing out white smoke.

A loud crack ripped through the air.

Then another. And another.

Rifle fire.

Tim dropped his head for cover, the grate clanging shut above him as several shots dinged off the rusty iron. Overhead, white smoke billowed throughout the room. Soon the gunfire began to die down, replaced by the sound of coughing and wheezing.

Tim drew a deep breath. It was time. Pushing up on the grate with all his strength, he flung it open and leapt out of the chamber and into the room. The smell of sulfur hung heavy in the air, and his eyes immediately began to itch from the smoke. After hundreds of times being exposed to it, the irritant was little more than an annoyance to him. The same could not be said for the others in the room. All about him, he could see the forms of scores of men stumbling around through the artificial mist.

Wasting no time, Tim charged forward, landing numerous blows as he moved through the mass of men. He punched them. He kicked them. He swept their legs out from under them. He grabbed hold of their clothing and threw them to the ground. There were so many of them that it would've been almost impossible *not* to hit one as he shot his hands and feet out in all directions. They must have been waiting out of sight of the drain, expecting him to arrive by that route. He had the upper hand now, but the smoke was already beginning to clear, and when it did, he would be in a most disagreeable situation.

According to *shinobi* protocol, it was already time for him to make his exit. A *shinobi* warrior could terrorize and overcome a much larger enemy force, but only so long as duplicity and surprise were on his side. Once his opponents recovered their bearings, the odds would be against him. It was unwise to linger much longer, but he could not leave yet. He might not get another chance at this, and he needed to find the Master. And so, against his better judgement, he continued to wade through the horde, fighting his way along in the dissipating smoke. But now the men began to fight back. One thrust the stock of a rifle at him. He ducked it and counterattacked with an uppercut to the man's face. He then reached back just in time to catch a hammer swinging toward his head. Twisting his torso, he locked up this second attacker's arm and leaned forward, throwing him to the ground.

As the smoke continued to clear, more and more men began to join in the attack. Tim needed to change tactics. He reached into his satchel and removed a dozen *shuriken* throwing stars. These he began hurling in rapid succession at his opponents' legs and feet as they charged him. The tiny blades stuck into flesh, tendons, and nerves, collapsing numerous attackers and greatly handicapping others.

A pair of men brandishing knives lunged at Tim as he was releasing the last of the *shuriken*. He sidestepped them and, reaching once more into his bag, produced a handful of *metsubushi* blinding powder, and flung it into their eyes. The two dropped their weapons and began rubbing at their faces with their shirt sleeves, trying to brush away the peppery mixture. Tim dropped low and swept their legs out from under them, knocking them to the ground. As he was rising again, a large assailant grabbed him from behind, forcing him into a chokehold. Tim responded by reaching back with both his hands and tightly grasping the sides of the man's head, while gouging his eyes with his thumbs. The man yelped and immediately let him go. Tim released his head and brought his own arms back into fighting position, from which he drove one elbow back into the chokeholder's sternum while swinging out with the other arm to deflect an incoming right hook.

Though Tim fought ever more furiously, the assailants, stepping over the fallen forms of their incapacitated comrades, continued to press in from all sides. The smoke had all but vanished, leaving him totally exposed to their onslaught. For the moment he held them at bay, but without recourse to more lethal means of defense, he would soon be overwhelmed. In the desperateness of the situation, the temptation to kill began once more to arise within him. He suppressed it. Better to die here than to live as the monster from his nightmares, he thought. And as the men continued to push forward with their assault, dying seemed like an ever more likely possibility.

"That's enough! Withdraw!"

Tim wasn't sure where the voice had come from, but he felt certain that he recognized it. The attackers, heeding the command, immediately ceased their assault and fell back several feet. Tim, now totally boxed in, likewise stopped fighting as he waited to see what would happen next. Several of the men in front of him shuffled aside to make way for whoever had issued the order. As that individual now came forward through their ranks, Tim's eyes widened slightly in recognition. It was "Arnold."

"Mr. Cratchit," Arnold said with a sneer, crossing his massive arms in front of his chest, "thank you for accepting our invitation."

Tim said nothing. Arnold eyed him up for a moment, then went on speaking.

"We were sorry to have to slaughter your employees, Mr. Cratchit, but it was necessary to show you how greatly we wanted you to visit us here. I hope their families will understand."

"So," Tim said, finally speaking, "*you're* the Master of the Order of the Hammer."

Arnold smiled, his large, toothy grin highlighted by his bright orange beard and mustache. "No," he responded.

"I am not. I am merely the right hand of the Master; the mouthpiece of the Master; the *servant* of the Master."

"I see," said Tim dryly. "So you're his lap dog." Arnold did not react to the provocation, but instead launched into what seemed to be a well-rehearsed diatribe.

"We are the Order of the Hammer," he bellowed. "You cannot stop us. No one can. The Master has given us our mission, and we shall carry it out, regardless of the human cost."

"Does this 'mission' include butchering innocent counting-house workers?" Tim interjected.

"It does," replied Arnold. "If the situation requires it."

"And have you no regard even for your own?" demanded Tim, his anger starting to grow.

"You speak of your brother," Arnold replied calmly. "Peter Cratchit died a noble death, carrying out the mission of the Order of the Hammer. He was not the first, and he will not be the last. A thousand more Peters . . . a *million* more Peters will perish before our mission is completed. No number of lives, and certainly no individual's life is more important than the success of our cause."

Tim glared at Arnold and fought to maintain control of his rage. If he gave into it now, he would surely kill the man, and that was something he could not allow himself to do.

"The world as you know it will burn," continued Arnold. "It will come crashing down around you. Everything you know. Everything you've loved. It will all be gone. A new order shall arise where the workman is supreme. Soon, the tyrants will fall. We will trample them under our feet. It does not matter how many innocents die along the way. Their lives will be like sweet incense offered up on the altar of our cause."

Tim clenched his teeth, trying to contain his growing hatred. He was in control. He would not kill. He would not kill.

No.

He *had* to kill.

He reached back and grasped his right hand about the hilt of his *katana*. As he did so, two of the closest thugs stepped forward to attack him. In one, fluid motion, he unsheathed his weapon and swung the blade down in a diagonal arc in front of him, slicing smoothly through the men's bodies as if they were made of warm butter. Time seemed to stand still as he felt the tiny droplets of their blood spattering upon the exposed portions of his face and hands. With grim satisfaction, he watched their startled faces as their eyes glossed over, and he listened without remorse to the gurgling sounds emitting from their throats as their severed torsos slumped to the ground before him.

Arnold smiled.

Tim raised his *katana* in a two handed grip up to his left shoulder, preparing for the next attack. Blood oozed down the edge of the blade and into the crevices of the emblazoned holly leaf. His eyes caught a glimpse of the little decoration, the red color highlighting it against the surrounding cold steel of the weapon. For one minuscule moment, the sight reminded him of his youth . . . of his family . . . of his vow. Then, at Arnold's command, several more Order members moved in to attack, and Tim's killer instinct took over completely.

For the first twenty minutes, the battle was like a dance, albeit a lethal one filled with severed limbs and agonized screams. While Tim's *shinobi* training taught him to avoid large-scale confrontations such as this, his mastery of finer swordsmanship gave him a relish for open battle. Now, his guilt drown out by pulsing adrenaline, he plunged into the fray without reserve. The Order members attempted to box him in, stabbing at him with their bayonets. They lunged forward, five, six, even eight at a time, trying to throw him off balance so that one of them might deliver a killing blow.

Tim's blade flashed in the bright light of the warehouse, appearing little more than a blur as he swung it about, easily parrying his opponents' weapons while following up with lethal strikes of his own. Three of the assailants raised their rifles, aimed them at his head, and squeezed the triggers. He dropped to one knee, and the projectiles ripped through the air over him, missing their intended target, yet still finding plenty of other flesh and bone in which to embed themselves.

"Cease firing!" yelled Arnold, "You're hitting each other! Stab him!"

The smoke from the discharged rifles wafted down around Tim, giving him a degree of concealment in his kneeling position. Gripping the handle of the *katana* with his left hand, he swung the blade along a horizontal path, making a perfect semi-circle from his right shoulder across the front of his body until his arm and the blade extended straight out from his left side. Half-a-dozen men crumpled to the ground around him, their legs sliced clean through just above the knees.

Tim rose to his feet and spread his legs into a wide fighting stance, lowering his center of gravity in order to better maintain his balance. The floor was beginning to grow slick with pooling blood, and not just that of his enemies.

There were too many of them. For every attacker he cut down, another stood ready to take his place on the line. While his limbs began to fatigue, his opponents came at him fresh for the fight. It was inevitable. As his reactions slowed, the bayonets began to find their marks. Though he still managed to knock them aside before they could penetrate to a lethal depth, their tips dipped into his skin with increasing frequency, tearing his flesh and sending sharp jolts of pain through his nerves. He clenched his teeth together and fought on. If this was the end, then so be it.

Blood dripping from his wounds, Tim raised his *katana* to deflect a large axe blade that came swinging down at his head from somewhere behind him. The force of the blow jarred his weakening arms. He barely managed to sidestep to the right in time to avoid another axe, which flew through the space he'd just occupied and cleaved into the chest of the first attacker with a sickening crunch. Another man rushed in from his right, driving a large maul toward his knees. Tim leapt over the weapon and swung his *katana* back with one hand, decapitating the assailant. Then he felt it. A bayonet pierced into the calf of his left leg. The blade penetrated several inches. He managed to eviscerate the owner, but stumbled back in pain after having done so. This was no flesh wound. The point of the bayonet snapped off and now protruded from his leg, blood oozing out from all around it.

The fighting stopped as the men fell back, waiting to see if Tim would collapse from his wound. He steadied himself, shifting most of his weight to his uninjured leg. The intense pain combined with the loss of blood made him swoon, but he gritted his teeth and held on to consciousness through force of will. The floor around him was awash in blood and littered with dozens of bodies. Standing at the center of the carnage, he eyed the rabble. The men glared back, their faces set with grim yet fanatical determination.

Tim inhaled deeply. He held his breath for a moment or two, and then let it loose with a fearsome battle cry, snapping his *katana* once more up over his head for the last stand. The Order members shouted back in unison and rushed in from all sides.

And then . . . fire.

There was fire all around him.

Tim wasn't immediately sure what had happened. The attackers in front of him dropped their weapons and scattered, rushing frantically about, their clothing aflame. No attackers connected with him from behind or from the sides, either. A loud cracking sound drew his attention to his right. There, standing amidst the flames and thick, black smoke, was some kind of . . . monster. As he watched, it finished smashing its way through the boarded-up front door, even as it continued spraying a glowing stream of molten, orange liquid from somewhere within its torso.

Tim had seen many strange things throughout his journeys, but never anything like this. The creature was large, probably about nine feet tall and six feet across at the shoulders. It looked to be made entirely of metal and had the appearance of a heavily armored European knight. As it moved further into the building, the stream of molten liquid continued to spray forth from within its chest cavity, dousing more of the men and setting them alight.

Screams of agony filled the air. The contraption stomped forward on two squat legs, causing the walls of the building to tremble as it moved. From behind it, a second machine entered the warehouse through the collapsed door. Identical to the first, this one also immediately set about covering the room in flame.

Many of the Order members were already dead. Others floundered about, screaming in pain as the fire consumed their flesh. Arnold yelled at them to rally, and several dozen did so. At Arnold's command, this group of survivors charged *en masse* at the mechanical beasts and set about hammering on the monsters with their axes and mauls. They pounded away with their weapons, yet succeeded only in making a few dents in the metal armor. The machines responded by thrusting the long spear tips on their arms through many of the men, skewering them like wild game.

Following Arnold's instructions, several Order members fell back into a line from which they opened fire with their rifles. The shots were worse than ineffective. They ricocheted off the machines' armor, striking and killing many of the men fighting in the melee.

By this time, three more of the contraptions had entered the warehouse through the collapsed door, bringing the total number to five. They roared about the place, wreaking havoc. Tim watched the massacre from the place on the ground where he'd fallen during the opening salvo. He'd twice narrowly managed to avoid being crushed by the machines' feet and now attempted to position the body of one of the fallen to shield himself from the intense heat overhead. The Order members had apparently forgotten all about him as they rushed to confront this new and much more lethal threat. Despite their efforts, Tim knew there was no way they were going to win this one. Scores of them already lay dead and burning all around the warehouse, yet they had not destroyed or even incapacitated a single one of the machines.

Arnold's shouts were barely audible over the agonized wails of his men and the deafening roar of the monsters. He was trying to rally the last of the Order members, but there were so few left. The ground shook as though there were an earthquake as the five contraptions pounded about the room, grinding the fallen into pulp upon the floor. Tim noticed that the stone walls were beginning to tremble ever more violently. It was time to get out of here.

His injured leg now totally numb, he crawled across the warehouse floor, dragging himself through sticky pools of coagulating blood and over heaps of piled corpses as dust from the pulverized mortar of the walls filled the air. No one tried to stop his progress. He reached the drain and threw himself into it, hitting the bottom just as his ears caught the sound of the first falling stones. The warehouse was coming down. He quickly rolled over onto his stomach and pulled himself into the tunnel that lead back to the river.

Tim inched his way through the tube on his elbows. Dust spilled into it from the collapsing building, choking him. Finally, he reached the end of the tunnel. Gripping the edges, he pulled himself out and fell into a pile of snow on the river's edge. He turned his head and looked back up. The building appeared to be entirely gone, the shoreline where it had once stood now shrouded in a veil of dust and falling snow.

Tim lay there on the bank of the river. Blood seeped out of his wounds, staining the snow around him. The cold wind whipped across his body. He tried to focus his mind—tried to hold on to consciousness, but he could not. He closed his eyes and drifted off.

CHAPTER 11

Tim awoke in significantly more comfortable surroundings than those he last remembered. He recalled losing consciousness along the frozen river behind the Order's warehouse, but now quite inexplicably found himself lying in a warm bed. Had he been captured? He glanced about. The little room was not familiar to him, and there was no one in sight. Where was he? How had he gotten here?

The room was sparsely furnished. Apart from the small bed upon which he was lying, there was only a little wooden table and a single chair, both of which sat on the other side of the room, about ten feet away to his left. He was pleased to see his *katana* and weapons pack resting upon the table top. Whoever had brought him here apparently had not felt it necessary to disarm him. Perhaps he'd not been captured after all. They'd even gone so far as to clean the blade of his *katana*, which now gleamed in the murky light filtering into the room from a solitary, soot-covered window. The walls around him were covered in plain, white plaster, which was cracked in several places, and other than the window, it appeared the only exit was a small, brown door on the wall opposite the one behind his head. Apart from the fact of his having no memory of how he got here, nothing seemed out of place.

Tim shifted his legs to sit up in the bed. Pain immediately shot through his entire body. He was in rough shape. His right leg in particular was extremely stiff and sore. Nevertheless, he was happy to find that someone had removed the bayonet tip from his calf and had cleaned and carefully bandaged the wound. Who could have done all of this, he wondered. Despite his curiosity, he didn't want to wait around to find out. Though there was no obviously hostile presence, he decided it would be prudent to get moving as soon as possible. Trust no one, the *shinobi* had taught him. To this end, he swung his legs over the side of the bed and, gritting his teeth, raised himself to his feet. The pain was severe. He stumbled and nearly fell, but managed to catch himself against the back wall. Steadying his legs, he began hobbling over to the table to retrieve his weapons.

He was about half way across the room when he heard a creaking sound. He stopped and looked over at the door. The knob was slowly turning. Someone was coming. As quickly as he could manage, he stumbled the rest of the distance to the table, reaching out for his *katana*. He grasped his hand about the hilt and raised his arm, bringing the blade up in front of his body as he turned to face the intruder.

"You really shouldn't be trying to walk yet, Mr. Cratchit."

Tim was taken aback. In the doorway stood a beautiful young woman. She was small, but had a strong build and was smartly dressed. Her blue eyes seemed to flicker at him in the hazy light of the room, and her perfect black hair was held up with a golden brooch that looked to be shaped like some sort of insect.

"Miss Wilkins, isn't it?"

"It is," she said with a smile. "I believe we met briefly at the theatre this past summer. You may call me Anna, if you'd like."

"I believe we did," said Tim, "though I prefer 'Miss Wilkins' for the time being."

"Good," she replied. "So do I."

Tim eyed her up and down. She was very beautiful, and there was something quite strong about her. He liked it. "You brought me here?" he finally asked.

"I did," she replied, smiling again. "And I can assure you it was not easy."

"How did you find me?" he inquired, his eyes narrowing with suspicion.

"Perhaps I just happened to be out walking along the river in the middle of the night, admiring the snow," she responded, her voice light and playful.

"Were you?" he asked, still suspicious.

"No," she replied, her voice becoming more serious as the smile faded from her face. "I wish it were as simple as that, but it's not." She hesitated for a moment, looking at him. "You're already deeply involved in all of this," she said at last. "It's time someone told you the truth."

Tim slowly lowered the *katana*. "The truth about what?"

She hesitated again, staring at him intently with those blue eyes, as if trying to determine whether she could trust him. "The truth about what happened last night," she finally said. "As you and everyone else in the city knows, my father, Richard Wilkins, is a very powerful man. Most don't realize how powerful. Several years back, he coordinated the formation of a clandestine organization known simply as the Association. This group is made up of a handful of wealthy and influential individuals, like my father. Their original purpose was to create a secret security force for the protection of their assets. It was meant to be an elite private army. Over time though, the plan evolved, and at my father's instigation eventually became the Juggernaut Project."

"So that's what I saw last night?" asked Tim. "Juggernauts?"

"Yes," she replied. "My father believed it was time to look for protection beyond traditional weapons. He's always been obsessed with the latest developments in science and technology. Unfortunately, in his mind this also includes dabbling in the occult. He became increasingly interested in spiritualism after the death of my mother. He's consulted with numerous seers and astrologers and now believes he has the means to ensoul the Juggernauts."

"Ensoul them?" Tim asked.

She sighed. "He intends to animate the machines by trapping lost souls within them."

Now Tim smiled, but only briefly. She gave him a stern look clearly meant to indicate the seriousness of the situation. He took the hint.

"How does he hope to accomplish this?" he asked her, turning the sides of his mouth down to ensure that he would not offend her again with a grin.

"He has an artifact . . . a Relic, which he believes is the key to arcane power. He thinks this object can serve as a channel for spiritual forces."

"And what is this object?" inquired Tim.

She turned her head slightly and gave him a sideways glance. "Mr. Cratchit," she said, raising her meticulously shaped eyebrows, "*you* knew Ebenezer Scrooge quite well, did you not?"

"I did know Mr. Scrooge," he replied, his curiosity piqued. "I might even say he was like a second father to me."

"Then you must know of his 'conversion', as people called it?"

"I know that he became a good man rather suddenly," Tim said.

"Do you know what brought about this change?" she asked

Tim furrowed his brow, giving her a quizzical look. "I can't say that I do," he admitted.

She smiled once more, her lips curving up gently in perfect symmetry. "Then you have not heard of the Spirits," she said. "Allow me to enlighten you. I know the story quite well. It happened many Christmas Eves ago . . ."

Tim found himself engrossed in the tale of Mr. Scrooge's ghostly visitors. He didn't quite believe the story, but he'd also never been able to think of a more reasonable explanation for his benefactor's sudden change in character.

What if it were true? What if Mr. Scrooge really had been haunted not only by three spirits, but by his deceased business partner, Mr. Marley? The idea was intriguing. Anna—he was already beginning to think of her as Anna—seemed to relish in telling the story. Clearly she'd heard it many times before from her father. Tim felt a connection with this girl, a warmness he'd not experienced for far too long. He needed to be on his guard. Trust no one, the *shinobi* had taught him. Trust no one.

"Earlier this week, my father's investigators finally recovered the door knocker," she said, wrapping up the story. "He is determined to use it as a medium for channeling the lost souls observed by Scrooge into the Juggernauts. He's convinced this will increase their power and guarantee their loyalty to himself alone."

Tim thought for a moment. "That is an . . . interesting story," he said. "I'm grateful that you shared it with me, and I'm equally grateful for everything you've done for me here." He paused slightly before continuing. "There's one thing I don't understand," he said. "Why are you helping me?"

"Because I need you," she replied, looking directly into his eyes. "I need a warrior of my own."

"I don't think I can help you," Tim said, meeting her gaze. "You see, I *am* warrior, but there's one crucial thing I can't do. I won't kill."

"Oh really?" she asked, again raising her eyebrows. "Well there seemed to be plenty of blood on your sword when I found it," she said, gesturing toward his *katana.*

Tim glanced at the weapon. Who was he trying to fool? It had only been a few hours since he'd massacred dozens of men, and while that had arguably been in self-defense, he didn't feel exceptionally guilty about it either.

"I know what those criminals from the Order of the Hammer did to your employees," Miss Wilkins said, stepping in closer toward him. "I know what they did to your brother."

He looked back into her eyes. They seemed to sparkle with a cold passion.

"My father and the Association have been tracking and fighting them for some time," she continued. "Last night they struck a devastating blow. They believe they even killed the alleged Master of the Order. Your brother has been avenged."

"I can't help you," Tim repeated, hoping to test her resolve.

She stepped back. "Mr. Cratchit," she said, her voice even, but still pleasant to hear. "Your old life is over. Your family is dead, your business destroyed. You have nothing left behind you. But I need you."

Tim had to admit, she raised some valid points. And she was quite attractive. Furthermore, she was offering him a chance to do what he did best. While he still didn't completely trust her, he had little to lose at this point. He decided to test her one last time.

"Why do you need me?" he asked. "You have the Juggernauts. They seem sufficient, to say the least. And if what you say is true, they will soon be even more so."

For the first time in their conversation, she frowned. "I need you *because* of the Juggernauts," she said. "I need you to stop my father."

Now Tim raised his eyebrows while Anna cast her gaze to the floor.

"I don't believe in his work," she continued, suddenly seeming quite vulnerable. "I fear he is heading toward disaster, toying with forces he cannot control. By doing so, he's threatening not only himself, but everyone and everything around him." She looked back at Tim, a stoic but pleading expression on her face. "I love him, and I want no harm to come to him, but he must be stopped before he ruins everything.

"You will be handsomely rewarded, of course," she added.

Tim stared at her, considering his options. "I'll do it," he said at last.

"Good," she replied with a faint smile. "And thank you." She took several paces back from him toward the door. "You may remain here in this safe house as long as you need.

I acquired it on my own when I was much younger. My father does not know about it."

"Thank you," Tim said. "And in what part of the city might this 'safe house' be located?"

"Camden Town," she replied. "Your . . . costume . . . is currently being washed and mended. I'll have a servant bring it over when it is ready. I suggest you put it back on. That night gown doesn't really suit you."

Tim felt slightly embarrassed, a most unusual sensation for him, as he remembered that he was not dressed. "Thank you," he said again.

"You're welcome, Mr. Cratchit," she replied. Then, giving him one last, lovely smile, she opened the door and departed.

CHAPTER 12

Wilkins watched as four of his technicians hoisted up the back end of one of the specially-built transportation wagons and slid the last of the Juggernauts into its proper place for the ceremony. Other workers hurried about, busying themselves with repairing dents and polishing the Juggernauts' exterior armor so that they seemed to glow a pale orange in the light of the simmering furnaces. Everything was almost perfect.

"Father, I still don't understand why you think we must go through with this."

Wilkins said nothing. Annabelle stood beside him in the foundry, watching with him as the technicians went about their work. He'd hoped his daughter would have simply accepted his judgement by now, but instead her objections had grown more frequent as the hour of ensoulment drew nearer. Not that it mattered greatly. The ceremony would commence tonight, with or without her approval. He did not need his child's permission for anything. Still, it would have been preferable for her to be at least partially convinced beforehand.

"We have crushed the Order of the Hammer," she continued. "The Juggernauts have proven once again to be effective as they now are. Why must we go through with this?" She gestured toward the machines and the men preparing them.

Wilkins answered her with silence. He waited until she began opening her mouth to speak again. "Do you believe the Order of the Hammer was our only enemy?" he asked, cutting her off before any further words could escape her lips. "Do you really think that our victory last night will be the end of our problems? Do you truly imagine that no one else will ever oppose us?"

"No father," she quickly replied. "But I . . ."

"There will always be enemies, Annabelle. And we must always be ready to meet them with vastly superior force. We can never be too prepared. We can never be too powerful. You must accept this."

"Father," she said, a bit more quietly, as if trying not to provoke him. "I do understand. But I still stand by my concerns, and I hope that you will give them more consideration."

Wilkins turned to face her. She looked up at him with pleading eyes, reminding him so much of her mother. "I don't mean to scold you, Annabelle," he said. "But what I am doing here tonight is of utmost importance for both of us. I have taken note of your concerns and have given them ample consideration. However, I must remind you that as long as I live, it is I who manages this Association. You may disagree with me as much as you'd like, but you will obey me nonetheless."

She cast her eyes down to the floor. "Yes, father," she said. "Of course."

"Look at me, Annabelle," Wilkins instructed her. She did so. "Soon," he said. "Very soon you will see the wisdom of my actions here. After tonight, we will be able to put this unpleasant division behind us. We will move forward together into a promising new future in which no one will ever dare oppose us again." He smiled at her. "The Relic truly is a panacea . . . but only if we make proper use of it. You will see."

"Very well, father," she said. "I accept your judgement. I promise you that this has been my last attempt to dissuade you."

"Good," he replied. "I am glad to hear it." He turned to look back at the Juggernauts. "Soon," he added. "Soon you will see."

"Yes, father," she replied.

Wilkins raised his hand in a sign of dismissal, and his daughter turned and walked out of the foundry. Long after the echoes of her footsteps had died away, he continued to watch the ongoing preparations, alone. He had no qualms, no doubts. Everything was proceeding according to his plan, and there was no reason to think that it would not continue to do so. Tonight was Christmas Eve. By morning, the Juggernauts would be ensouled, and then they would be unstoppable. Then let ten Orders of the Hammer rise up against him—let a hundred Orders of the Hammer rise up against him—it would no longer matter.

Wilkins reached up and placed his right hand over his chest, feeling the Relic beneath his starched white shirt. The chain on which the artifact hung pulled heavily on the back of his neck and was most uncomfortable, but he refused to allow his prize to be stored in any other place. He had come too far and was too close to victory to entrust the source of his power to anyone else. His consultants had warned him that he must maintain control of the Relic at all times, for whoever possessed the Relic would have command of the spirits, and, by extension, command of the Juggernauts.

It seemed such a simple thing, he thought, but his consultants had assured him that it was anything but. By laying her hands upon it, one of his seers had been able to obtain visions of its tremendous history. She explained to Wilkins that the metal from which it had been crafted came from the blade used to execute King Charles I at the culmination of the English Civil War over two centuries earlier. It had tasted royal blood. Now, as it had taken a king out of the mortal world, so it would serve to make Wilkins king of the spirit world. How ironic that the source of unlimited power had sat unrecognized for years beneath the nose of his old competitor, Ebenezer.

His thoughts now drifted to his former friend. They had been close, he and Scrooge. There was no denying that. Even during their rivalry over Belle, they'd remained on good terms. But then their periods of apprenticeship had ended, and they'd gone their separate ways. Wilkins had obtained Belle, just as he'd always desired, but Scrooge achieved something better—success. While Wilkins scoffed at Scrooge and his miserly ways at every possible opportunity, he had to admit that Ebenezer had proven himself a successful man of business—much more so than he himself had initially been. As he'd been forced to spend every farthing he earned feeding and clothing his growing family, Scrooge had hoarded his money like a raven. The man had been a fool, but he'd been a wealthy fool. If only

Wilkins could have had a fraction of Scrooge's fortune, what great uses he could have put it to!

It wasn't until Belle's death that he'd gotten the chance to amass his own tremendous wealth. That was over twenty years ago now. Poor woman. She'd died giving birth to Annabelle, and it had broken his heart. He'd been left with neither the woman he loved nor with any money, all while Scrooge sat on his pile of ill-gotten gain. After a brief period of intense mourning, he'd thrown himself entirely into his work, determined to overtake his old fellow apprentice. With Belle no longer at his side, he felt freer to act more ruthlessly in the pursuit of gain, and it had paid off very well for him. With countless new acquisitions each year, he'd built his empire link by link and yard by yard. True, he'd also made great sacrifices to protect and preserve it, not the least of which was the lives of his own sons. And now here he stood, on the brink of unlimited power, while Ebenezer lay rotting in his grave. A fitting end to their rivalry, he thought as he caressed the Relic. Yes, everything was proceeding according to plan.

CHAPTER 13

Tim wasn't sure what had drawn him back to this place, but he'd known that he'd needed to come. Now he stood once more in the churchyard, looking down upon his father's grave, almost as if he expected the stone marker to speak to him, to confirm that he was making the appropriate decision. It remained stubbornly silent.

So much had changed over the course of the last 24 hours. When he'd come home from the Far East several months earlier, he'd been determined to start a new life for himself. He'd hoped to put away his martial skills and re-forge his relationship with his father, with some vague hope of regaining the life he'd left behind when he'd gone abroad.

But then his father had died. He'd tried to follow in the man's footsteps and had made some initial efforts to take an active role in the running of his firm, but the call of the warrior's life had been too strong. As the months passed, he'd gradually found himself spending less time at his desk and more time skulking in the shadows of forsaken sections of the city, seeking opportunities to hone his already considerable fighting prowess.

And then Peter had been killed. And now all of his employees. The destruction of the counting house seemed to him like the final page in a past chapter of his life, or perhaps rather like the end of a short intermission between the two stages of his life as a *shinobi* warrior. Granted, the business could be rebuilt and new workers hired, but the massacre still had a somber note of finality about it.

There had also been the breaking of his vow. He'd killed so many men at the Order's warehouse fortress. He'd decapitated them; gutted them; slashed off their limbs. Of course they'd given him little choice. If he hadn't killed them, they'd have butchered him like the murderers they were. It had been self-defense—arguably. But now Anna—Miss Wilkins—wanted him to assassinate her own father. This was harder to justify. If what she said was true, the whole city and perhaps the entire country were in danger. Still, there was a difference between killing men while defending oneself in battle and deliberately seeking out an elderly gentleman with the sole purpose of ending his life.

Tim knew he'd already made his decision. His vow was broken. There was no going back. He would at some point need to seek a dispensation, but there wasn't time now. The sun was already beginning to set, and Anna had warned him that the ceremony would be taking place shortly after the onset of darkness. Along with his mended *gi*, her servant had carried instructions on how to find the location where the ritual would be held.

As Tim stood at his father's final resting place, his ears detected the sound of footsteps crunching through the snow toward him. His first thought was that Miss Wilkins had found him, but as he listened, he realized the steps were falling too heavily to be hers. It had to be a man, and one of considerable weight.

Especially after the hostile encounters of the last several days, Tim knew he needed to be on his guard. He continued listening as the individual drew closer, but pretended not to notice him. The pace of the steps remained constant as they grew louder by the moment. Finally, when the mysterious intruder sounded to be about ten paces back, Tim turned to face him.

It was Arnold. Or what was left of him. Tim dropped his arms to his sides and positioned his feet shoulder width apart, assuming an upright, natural fighting stance, though he did not expect the wreck of a man standing before him to put up much of a fight.

Arnold stopped advancing and looked up at him. Tim eyed his opponent up and down. How he'd survived at all, Tim could not fathom, but it was a severe understatement to say that he had not escaped the warehouse unscathed. The right half of his face was scorched beyond recognition, the eye socket on that side a mere gaping hole. His beard and mustache were almost completely burnt off, with only scattered blackened hairs sticking up here and there from his chin. His clothes were largely burnt away and his body covered in oozing blisters and peeling, purple skin. Even from this distance, the smell of ash was still strong on him.

"Mr. Cratchit," Arnold mumbled in a raspy voice. His words were badly slurred, as his lips were swollen and apparently fused together on the right side.

Tim almost felt bad for the man. Almost. "Have you come to beg me to put you out of your misery?" he asked.

Arnold shook his head, grimacing with the good half of his mouth. "No," he coughed. "I have come to warn you."

"Warn me about what?" Tim asked as he tightened his fists, fully expecting some form of treachery at any moment.

"I've come to warn you," choked Arnold, "about the Master."

"Your Master is dead," Tim replied, though he now had his doubts. After all, until a minute ago, he'd believed that Arnold too had perished in the attack.

"No." said Arnold. "The Master lives. That is why I have come to warn you. The Master betrayed us, and she will also betray you."

Tim looked at Arnold, his eyes widening. "She?"

CHAPTER 14

Clinging to the underside of a coach as it made its way through the wet, sloppy streets was definitely not Tim's favorite way to travel, but the steel foundry Miss Wilkins had listed as his target was on the far northern end of the city, and he needed to conserve his strength for what would in all likelihood be an even more grueling night than the one before. The coach itself belonged to one Mr. Niles, whom Miss Wilkins had identified as a member of the Association. Of all the members, his home had been the nearest to the churchyard and therefore the most convenient from which to catch a ride. Now, as Tim jostled back and forth to the sound of clicking hooves, he pondered the latest development of the evening.

Could it be true? Could it really be that Miss Wilkins herself had been the face behind the Order of the Hammer? Arnold had seemed very sincere when he made this revelation, and what reason would a dying man have to lie? If he were in earnest, then it was Anna who was responsible for Peter's death. And now Tim was working for her. The thought disgusted him. He had attempted to question Arnold in the churchyard, but it was of no use. His injuries had been too severe, and he'd died shortly after relaying his troubling news.

Tim's thoughts were cut short by the coach's arrival at the foundry. As the vehicle began to slow down, he dropped to the street and, lying flat on his back, allowed the rear axle to pass over him. Still prone, he rolled off the street, through the melting snow, and into some brambles on the side opposite the foundry. From the cover of the thorny brush, he gazed up at the building, scanning for a good point of entry. It was a massive structure, a perfect representation of industrial might. The brick wall in front of him had to be nearly 1,500 feet from end to end and thirty feet from top to bottom. A line of windows running along the entire upper portion of the wall glowed with an orange light, highlighting the steel bars that covered them, set just inches apart. Above the windows, at least two dozen round chimneys jutted up from the roof and into the night sky, appearing much like a row of obelisks marking the gateway to some forbidden tomb. Smoke wafted out of the majority of these, indicating that the furnaces beneath them were still simmering and probably hot enough to not only incinerate Tim in an instant, but even to melt all of his steel weapons.

The windows, he decided, would be his preferred means of entry, but he would need to file through at least three of the steel bars before he could get inside. There wasn't time for this. He was already behind schedule due to his delay in the churchyard.

He surveyed the roof. Most of the chimneys would be death traps, but it appeared that at least two of them were not releasing any smoke. Perhaps their furnaces had not been used today and would be cool enough to enter. Only closer investigation could tell.

Still kneeling in the brush, Tim unslung his bag and dug inside it, finding and removing his pair of *shuko* climbing claws. Even with small strips of cloth wrapped around them for insulation, the metal sucked the warmth from his hands as he pulled the devices on over his palms and looped their fasteners about his wrists. With the claws securely in place and his bag once more over his shoulder, he darted across the street, leaving the cover of the brambles for the shadows of the towering walls. Within moments he was making his ascent, grinding the four spikes of each claw into the mortar between the bricks as he worked his way to the top.

Peering cautiously over the roof from its edge, Tim thought he saw movement in the shadows of the fourth chimney from him. As he looked and listened more closely, he could confirm that there were two sentries present, though it didn't appear as though they were taking their job very seriously. Maybe they didn't expect any trouble this evening. They certainly weren't looking for it, as they were standing near each other, chatting and chuckling in hushed tones. Still, Tim couldn't risk having them spot him and sound the alarm.

He climbed slowly over the edge of the wall and onto the roof, being careful not to make any sound. Crouching to maintain a low profile, he removed the *shuko* claws and reached once more into his satchel, this time producing three large wooden straws. These he fitted together to assemble one of his favorite *shinobi* weapons, a blowgun. The darts were equipped with a powerful sedative that would keep the guards unconscious until well after his work here was done.

Having loaded the weapon, Tim pointed it at the neck of the sentry who was least visible, partially concealed behind one of the chimneys. A second after he blew on the end of the pipe, the man let out an audible yelp and slapped at his neck. His companion looked about frantically, but apparently did not have the sense to immediately seek cover. Within a minute, both were slumped over on the roof where they would stay for a good, long time.

With the immediate threat of detection eliminated, Tim disassembled his blowgun and, while still being careful to maintain a low profile, made his way across the roof, darting between the towering chimneys until he reached one that appeared to be inactive. The smooth, black metal felt cool to the touch, an encouraging sign. After double-checking to ensure that his *katana* was mounted securely on his back, he stretched out his arms and wrapped them as far as possible around the chimney's base. They didn't quite reach half the circumference, but it would be enough. Lifting his legs, he pressed his inner thighs against the cold metal and began to shimmy his way up. Once at the top, he stared down the long, narrow tube leading into the building. There was no sign of any flame, nor did he feel any significant amount of heat. It would be safe. Well . . . comparatively safe.

Without any more hesitation, he gripped the wide lip of the chimney top with both hands and lowered himself into the tube. It was a snug fit, but he could make it. With his hands and feet pressed firmly against the sides, he started his descent. The interior of the chimney was caked with soot that crumbled as he moved, making it difficult to maintain traction. He had to be careful. If he slipped, he'd go all the way to the bottom, and his landing would be less than graceful. It would be difficult enough fighting any interior guards with his injured calf, let alone two broken legs.

The going was slow, but Tim eventually reached the bottom, lowering himself gently from the chimney into the furnace until he stood in cool, knee-deep ashes. The unit within which he found himself had apparently not been used for some time, though even here he could feel the dry heat that permeated the entire outer room, sucking the moisture from his exposed skin. Luckily, the doors of the furnace had been left partially open, giving him a good view of much of the vast interior of the foundry. There was plenty to see. Huge, black furnaces lined the far wall opposite him, heaps of coal glowing brightly inside of them, casting an orange light through the seams of the closed doors.

At the center of the room, about thirty feet away from him, several Juggernauts—he counted ten—stood dark and motionless in a semi-circular formation. Men in white laboratory jackets moved quickly amongst them, probably making the final preparations for the ensoulment ceremony.

In front of the Juggernauts stood a cluster of individuals, all of them well dressed. There were nine of them, eight men and one young woman. Tim recognized Anna immediately. She stood at the side of an elderly gentleman who had to be her father, Richard Wilkins. The only other person Tim recognized was Mr. Niles, though he assumed that the others were the rest of the Association members. As he watched, he noticed that Anna glanced about from time to time. She was probably trying to find some evidence of his presence, as the hour of ensoulment was growing dangerously near. Undoubtedly she expected him to have arrived by now, and so he would have if it had not been for the enlightening detour through the churchyard. Tim studied her. Could it really be that she was the evil mastermind Arnold had described? He would likely find out soon enough.

As Tim watched, the white-jacketed men apparently finished up with whatever it was they'd been working on. At a word from Mr. Wilkins, they vacated the foundry, leaving the Association members and Anna standing alone before the Juggernauts. This was it, Tim thought.

With his technicians gone, Mr. Wilkins stepped forward from the gathering and approached the silent Juggernauts, as if intending to address them. With his back turned to the other members, he reached up and began moving his hands over his chest, as though he were unbuttoning his shirt. At first Tim couldn't quite make out what the man was doing, but then he saw it. Wilkins reached within his shirt and pulled out a large, iron ring. It was the Relic. He gazed down upon it for a moment or two, a smile spreading over his face. Then he turned about to face the Association members, and as he did so, he lifted the iron ring over his head with both hands. His movement was so sudden that Anna and the Association members all instinctively took a step back.

"It is time!" Wilkins cried out. It seemed to Tim that he was not addressing the Association members, but neither was he speaking to himself. It was almost as though he were directing his words to the Relic itself. As he spoke, he slowly lowered the iron ring down upon his head, as if it were some sort of crown.

Tim watched, amazed, as the ring began to glow upon Wilkins' brow. The dull metal appeared to take on a sickly, greenish hue, like a bad lobster in a dark cellar. With each passing moment, the light grew brighter until there was no mistaking it for a trick of the imagination. Soon it shone like a halo about Wilkins' head.

Even more peculiar than the light itself was the noise that accompanied it. As the glow increased, the room became filled with a piteous wailing sound that could only be described as the moans of unnumbered lost souls. It was absolutely unnerving. Tim tore his gaze from the sight and looked back at the little cluster of Association members. They all appeared to be at least as unsettled as he was. Anna's eyes were fixed wide open. Mr. Niles was trembling violently. Even a large, hulk of a man that dwarfed the rest of them took another step backward.

Anna looked about rapidly, no doubt wondering why her warrior had not yet arrived. As the Association members continued to fall back, she began to move forward. Tim guessed that she intended to take matters into her own hands. Whether or not she was playing him as yet another pawn, he needed to act now or it would be too late for all of them.

Covered in a thick layer of soot, Tim stepped out of the furnace and unsheathed his *katana*. There was no time for diversionary tactics. He would make a head-on assault and decapitate Richard Wilkins before any of the Association members could intervene.

Having decided upon this course of action, he leaned forward, braced his toes upon the stone floor, and was off like a shot, rushing silently through the hot, dry air toward his target. Someone shouted something—probably a warning to Wilkins—but Tim was too focused on his prey to make out the words. By the time Wilkins turned to face him, he was already leaping through the air, his *katana* raised up over his left shoulder in preparation for the killing blow. The setup couldn't have been more perfect. As Tim landed, he brought the blade swinging down in a wide arc toward Wilkins' neck. It passed through easily—too easily. Tim, unprepared for the lack of resistance, crashed to the floor, barely managing to break his fall with a well-timed somersault.

Laughter filled the air, magnified by the cavernous interior of the foundry. Tim turned around. Before him stood Richard Wilkins, his head still very much upon his shoulders and his entire body aglow with the greenish light. The deep laughter issuing from his throat seemed almost unearthly. Certainly it was much fuller and louder than what Tim would have expected from someone of so advanced an age—especially from someone who should now be dead.

"So," Wilkins boomed, his voice almost giddy. "You must be one of the last of the Order of the Hammer come to take your revenge. I welcome you. It pleases me that you are here tonight to witness my absolute triumph."

While Wilkins spoke, Tim slid his left hand into his bag and removed a small throwing knife. With a flick of his wrist, he hurled it at the glowing figure. The projectile sailed through the air and, before Tim's very eyes, passed harmlessly through the old man's face and clattered to the floor on the other side of the foundry.

Wilkins let out another laugh, even more maniacal than the one before. "Your weapons cannot harm me now," he bellowed. "Nothing can. I am invincible."

"Everyone has a weakness," Tim declared, trying to bide his time while he thought of an alternative plan.

Wilkins laughed again. "Everyone but me," he growled. "Still," he continued, "I cannot have you interrupting my ceremony." He nodded at the large

Association member Tim had noticed earlier. "Riggens, deal with him."

The giant of a man was surprisingly fast for his size. He lunged at Tim and caught hold of his right arm, squeezing it so hard that he was forced to drop his *katana*. Tim counterattacked, driving the extended second knuckles of his left hand into the soft tissue between Riggens' ribs. The blow had no effect. Riggens caught Tim's other arm and pulled him in close against his massive chest. He squeezed down hard, forcing the air out of Tim's lungs. Tim fought with all his strength to wriggle away, but he couldn't budge. He began to grow dizzy, and knew he would soon black out. Then it would be over.

In this half-conscious state, Tim wasn't sure whether he could trust his own senses. Was it a hallucination from the lack of oxygen, or did he really see wisps of greenish light now shooting out from the Relic? The little orbs seemed to circle about the room, and as they did so, the wailing continued to grow louder. Tim looked up as one of the sprites passed overhead. He was sure he could see within it the form of a face, its expression twisted in the most vulgar way, as if conveying untold anguish.

The lights continued to circle overhead, moving faster and faster. Then, with all the energy of an impassioned preacher, Wilkins threw both of his arms up into the air. He spoke no words, but Tim could almost feel him *willing* the spirits into the Juggernauts, and the spirits obeyed. All ten of them shot down from the ceiling and took up positions floating in front of the Juggernauts' closed chest cavities. Here they hovered for a moment before disappearing, fading back through the heavy metal doors.

At first, nothing happened. Silence filled the room. Wilkins trembled with apparent expectation. Then, the eye slits in the Juggernauts' helms began to glow with the greenish light. A wide, twisted smile spread across Wilkins' face. "Come to me, my warriors," he ordered them.

The Juggernauts obeyed the command. All ten of them stepped in toward Wilkins in perfect unison. Their movements were accompanied by no loud, mechanical sounds, nor did any heat emanate from them. Most significantly, no technicians guided their steps. They were powered entirely by the spirits, and those spirits answered only to Wilkins, the keeper of the Relic.

The animation of the Juggernauts came as a bit of a shock to everyone in the room, including Mr. Riggens. He loosened his crushing hold on Tim for just an instant, and an instant was all Tim needed. He dropped down and slipped out of Riggens' grip, helped in no small part by the thick layer of slippery ash that covered his *gi*. Upon the floor, he used his hands to propel himself back under his opponent's legs. Once behind the giant, he leapt up onto his back and caught his head in a chokehold. Riggens tried to pry him off, but Tim held on tight, wrapping his legs around the man's torso. He squeezed down on his neck with all his might, cutting off the blood supply to Riggens' brain. Within a few moments Riggens swayed, lost consciousness, and crashed to the floor.

The sound of his associate's body thunking on the ground drew Wilkins' attention back to Tim. He turned away from the Juggernauts to face the *shinobi* intruder once more. "So," he said, "you still think that you have a chance of defeating me?"

Tim did not answer.

Wilkins sneered. "Very well," he said. "I would like to honor you by allowing you to be the first person destroyed by my *new* Juggernauts."

At these words, the Juggernauts turned to face Tim. The doors of their chest cavities began to open outward, but this time there was no roaring fire within. In its place, the ghastly green light swirled about, looking very much to Tim like a tangled mass of ethereal serpents. He leapt backward with all the strength his aching legs could muster just as the Juggernauts commenced with their attack. Ghostly beams of light shot out from the behemoths' chests, striking where Tim had just been standing. While he managed to evade them, the unconscious Mr. Riggens was not quite so fortunate. Three of the rays struck his body, disintegrating him in an instant. Or perhaps it would be more accurate to say they *aged* him in an instant. In the space of about two seconds, he grew decades older, shriveled up, and rotted to dust.

Wilkins let out another chilling laugh. It seemed clear to Tim that the old man's sanity was slipping further by the moment.

"Allow me to present you with a gift," Wilkins cried out with a smirk. "The gift of death. A Merry Christmas to you." He pointed a finger at Tim. "Destroy him," he commanded the Juggernauts.

As Tim leapt away again, narrowly avoiding the death beams, he noticed a hand—a feminine hand—reaching up behind Wilkins. As he tumbled sideways, he caught a glimpse of Anna standing behind her father. She must have sneaked up on him while he was distracted by Riggins' fall. Now she carefully closed her left hand about the Relic and raised it a few inches, removing it from her father's brow. Tim observed the shocked expression on Wilkins' face as he suddenly stopped glowing and turned around to see who had dared to take his prize. In that instant, Anna dropped to one knee, snatched Tim's *katana* from the floor, and drove it up into her father's chest, burying it so deeply that the blade emerged from his back.

Wilkins gasped loudly. "Anna!" he cried. "Why?"

"I'm sorry, father," she replied coldly, "but I'm doing what must be done to ensure our family's legacy."

"You . . . you are my daughter . . . my heir," he gurgled, his voice already beginning to fade. "Why . . . why have you done this?" He slumped to the floor.

Anna, even with her petite stature, now towered above the dying figure, appearing very much to enjoy finally being in a position of control over him. "You always taught me," she said "that money can buy power, but only if one uses it to do so. I've come to understand that family can also be a key to power . . . but only if one makes use of it to that end. You knew this yourself, didn't you? That's why you killed my brothers. You found it necessary. And now I have found *this* necessary."

Wilkins moaned something as he feebly shifted his body on the floor, but the words were inaudible.

"I was content to wait in your shadow until you died," Anna continued. "The more power you amassed before your death, the more I could claim as my own once you were in your grave." She smiled. "I even hired a soldier of fortune to recruit desperate workmen and organize them into the Order of the Hammer so that you would be convinced to build yourself a private army . . . an army which I intended to employ against your lecherous associates. Yes, father, everything was proceeding well, and we might have parted on peaceful terms. But then you found the Relic. I could not risk that you would discover some way to use its power in order to prolong your own life indefinitely. After all of my considerable efforts, I refused to be cheated out of what is rightfully mine."

Wilkins' glossy eyes were fixed on Anna, but he was no longer groaning. Or moving. Or breathing.

Anna frowned. "I will *not* be cheated out of what is rightfully mine," she said again, her voice stern. "And now," she continued, looking up, her eyes meeting Tim's, "*this* is mine."

Tim watched as she raised the Relic above her own head. She *was* the Master. Peter's blood, his employees' blood—it was all on her hands. And now only he could stop her. Reaching into his pack, he removed another throwing knife and let it fly. The blade whizzed through the air and hit its mark, piercing through back side of Anna's right hand. She cried out in pain and dropped the Relic to the ground. The iron ring landed on its side with a dinging sound and rolled away into the darkness, landing somewhere between two of the simmering furnaces.

"What have you done?" Anna screamed at Tim as she clutched at her bloodied hand, the tip of the knife protruding through her palm. "You fool! We're all going to die!"

No sooner had she said these words than the Juggernauts, which until now had stood silently by, started to move about of their own accord, free from any control whatsoever. Ghastly green beams shot out in quick succession from their chests, methodically targeting anything that lived.

The Association members had begun to flee once Anna struck down her father, but the foundry was large, and they were just now reaching the pair of doors at the end of it. If only they'd left a moment sooner, they might have survived. Instead, one by one, they were hit with the rays and blasted into fine powder. Mr. Niles was the last of them to perish. He sat where he'd fallen, his back against one of the doors, his arms raised over his head, trying to shield himself. He continued to beg for mercy until the greenish light raked over him and he was no more.

At the same time the Association members were being annihilated, Tim and Anna had troubles of their own. They too were living creatures, and the Juggernauts seemed intent upon remedying this. The ground shook beneath them as three of the monstrous machines stomped about, targeting them with the glowing beams. The flashes of greenish light cast eerie, otherworldly shadows about the room, like something from a nightmare. Tim tucked and rolled to avoid one blast, then flipped backward to dodge another. He landed near Wilkins' corpse. His *katana* was still stuck in the old man's chest, buried so deeply that only the portion of the blade emblazoned with the holly leaf remained visible, protruding just below his heart. If he was to die here—and that seemed likely—he at least wanted to die like a warrior, with a weapon in his hand. He grasped the hilt of the sword and yanked upward, pulling it loose from Wilkins' flesh. It was not a moment too soon. As he leapt, a glowing beam struck the deceased, disintegrating his corpse. While Tim was retrieving his weapon, he caught glimpses of Anna doing her best to avoid her own obliteration. Still clutching at her hand, she ran zig-zag patterns about the room, narrowly staying ahead of the destructive rays. Tim knew that she couldn't keep it up forever. With each blast, the Juggernauts zeroed in on her.

Good. She deserved to die. She'd killed her father. She'd killed the Order members. She'd killed Peter. And now, she would be killed. It seemed fitting. Yet despite the sense of satisfaction Tim enjoyed at the thought of her imminent execution, there was a part of him that yet felt some inexplicable attachment to her. She was ruthless, true. And also crafty. And deceptive. Much like a true *shinobi*.

Very well, Tim decided. He would help the girl, if for no other reason than to go down fighting. Tumbling away from yet another death ray, he rushed across the floor toward one of the hotter furnaces. The doors were partially open and an intense heat radiated out. Raising his *katana* over his head with both hands, he plunged the blade down into the simmering coals, then immediately ducked to avoid another ghostly beam. Crouched down on the ground, he watched as the steel of the perfectly tempered blade began to grow red hot in the flames. Reaching out, he snatched up the weapon and pulled it from the simmering embers. The cord-wrapped hilt burnt his hand, but it was still possible to hold. On the opposite end, the last two feet of the blade glowed with a bright orange light.

Tim looked across the room. Anna was tiring, her pace slowing as two of the Juggernauts closed in on her. It was now or never. With all the speed his wounded body could muster, he began racing across the great room toward the Juggernaut closest to Anna. Like an avenging angel, he launched himself from the ground and leapt up into the air behind the metallic beast, swinging his fiery blade along a wide, horizontal arc, its path traced through the air by a trail of bright orange light. The burning weapon passed through the base of the Juggernaut's helm, severing it from its body. As Tim landed, the monster's head tipped backward, rolled off its shoulders and clanged loudly onto the floor.

Tim glanced down at his weapon. The blade was slightly bent from the force of the blow and was cooling rapidly. It had served its purpose but was ruined and useless to him now.

"Behind you!" Anna yelled.

Tim rolled away as one of the incandescent beams hit the ground where he'd just been standing. As he looked up, he saw the source of the attack. The decapitated Juggernaut lumbered toward him, preparing to target him again. He hadn't even slowed it down. Could nothing stop them?

Anna cried out to him again. "Get the Relic!"

Tim looked back at her. She had stopped moving. Behind her, a Juggernaut lined itself up for a lethal strike. Tim took a step in her direction. "The Relic!" she yelled again, as the Juggernaut fired its deadly ray.

Tim leapt at Anna, caught hold of her good hand, and slid to the floor, pulling her clear of the beam. Or nearly clear of it. The greenish light barely brushed over her ankle. Lying on the ground, Tim stared into her face. He could see the terror in her eyes as she rapidly aged—her beauty fading in an instant—and melted into dust in his grip.

Tim was momentarily stunned, unsure of how to take this new loss. Then a loud banging sound grabbed his attention. He looked across the room and noticed that the majority of the Juggernauts were gathered on the far side and were now pounding on the large, double steel doors at the front entrance, trying to get outside. If they were allowed to escape, they would find their way into the city, wreaking unimaginable destruction and killing hundreds or even thousands of innocent people.

It was up to Tim to end this, but he'd expended the last of the energy from his wounded body in attempting to take down the now-headless Juggernaut. His nerves, especially those in his leg, were on fire, screaming out for him to let his weary and damaged limbs rest. Everything depended on his next actions, but he didn't see how he would even be able to take them. Opening his hand to release the rest of Anna, he closed his eyes and, for the first time in many years, he prayed. "God help us," he whispered. "All of us."

These words fresh upon his lips, Tim arose and, pushing back the excruciating pain, began making a wild dash across the room, heading for the furnaces behind which the Relic had rolled. The three Juggernauts, only two of whom had heads, pounded after him, as if they sensed his intention. Their rays closely followed him all the way across the floor, growing more accurate with each strike. Jumping, tucking, and rolling, he passed between two of the furnaces and dropped to his hands and knees, feeling around frantically in the darkness. Then his hands seized upon it. The iron ring felt extraordinarily cool in his grip, as if it had just been pulled from the depths of the sea. Raising it above his head with his right hand, he emerged from the dark crevice and stood face to face with the Juggernauts.

"Stop!" he yelled aloud.

The room became silent. Tim sensed the power of the Relic pulsing through him. It was alluring. He could *feel* the Juggernauts, as though they were extensions of his own body. He was in total control, and moment by moment he was beginning to enjoy it. Images began to flow through his mind depicting all of the incredible things he could accomplish if he maintained mastery over this power for himself. Nobody would dare oppose his will. He could be rich beyond anything he'd even dared to imagine in the past. Kings would bow before him. Entire nations would offer their homage.

So, he thought, this is how men are driven mad.

He focused all of his concentration on the Juggernauts, desiring for them to come to him. Though he spoke no words, they understood. Those that had just earlier finished breaking down the foundry door and had begun to make their way outside now pounded with their heavy, rhythmic footsteps over to him. In his mind, he envisioned them all standing in a circle, facing inward, surrounding him. The Juggernauts, aware of his will and forced to obey it, moved themselves into this very formation, as if he had placed them there with his own hands.

Such control. Such power.

The images in Tim's mind grew more intense. Voices now whispered to him. With the power of the Juggernauts, he could do *anything*. He could be a god.

"You will obey me," Tim said aloud, though he knew there was no reason for him to do so. With his fist clenched so tightly about the Relic that his knuckles began to turn white, he raised it once more over his head. For the first time, he could feel the spirits resisting. He fought back, and they submitted to his will. They had no choice, for he held the Relic.

In one, fluid motion, the Juggernauts raised their arms and pointed their razor-sharp spears at one another. Then, they attacked. The sound of steel being ripped to shreds echoed loudly throughout the foundry as spear tips pierced through plated armor, riveted seams were torn open, and mechanical joints were smashed to pieces. The tremendous screeching noise was agony to Tim's ears, yet he forced himself to stay focused, guiding the Juggernauts fratricidal blows. The first of the ten crumpled to the ground, its squat legs gouged through so thoroughly that they could no longer support its massive weight. As it hit the floor, its chest began to glow. A greenish wisp morphed out of the light and floated up into the air where it resumed its earlier course, circumnavigating the ceiling, shrieking loudly as it sped along. Soon it was joined by another. And another. Finally, ten wisps circled the foundry, their awful wails enough to haunt a man for the rest of his life.

Tim looked down upon the devastated Juggernaut shells that surrounded him. The carnage was complete. They'd be good for nothing but scrap. Only one thing remained to be done. Walking over to the furnace in which he had earlier heated his *katana*, he reached his arm out over the glowing cinders. Taking one last look at the Relic, he released his grip, letting the iron ring fall into the burning coals. It impacted with a crackling sound, sending up a shower of orange sparks.

The spirits' wailing immediately began to grow more intense. Without looking up at them, Tim stepped over to the side of the furnace and placed his hands on the wooden handle of the large bellows there. Pulling down with all his strength, he began to pump the bellows, forcing oxygen into the coals, stoking the great fire.

The iron ring took on an orange glow and began to hiss as it grew hotter by the moment. The wisps circled the room faster and faster, their shrieking growing louder and louder. Then, they began to descend toward the furnace. They did not go willingly. Tim could see that they pulled back, fighting with all of their strength against whatever mysterious force dragged them downward toward the inferno. Their struggle was for naught. One by one, they were sucked into the blaze. A geyser of red-hot sparks spewed into the air, illuminating the room so brightly that the entire foundry seemed to be aflame. Tim fell backward onto the floor to avoid being scorched. A unified, horrible, deathly scream escaped the furnace and then . . . nothing.

The shower of sparks vanished with the last wail, and a wave of cool air flowed across the room. Tim climbed to his feet, then walked over to the furnace and peered inside. The fire had gone out entirely, leaving only black ashes behind. There was no trace of either the spirits or the Relic.

He looked back over his shoulder and glanced about the foundry. It was silent as the grave, for a grave it now was. The other furnaces still glowed orange, casting their eerie light throughout the room. By it, he could see the scattered piles of dust that marked the places where the Association members had met their ends. Near one pile—which mere minutes ago had been the most beautiful and treacherous woman he'd ever known—lay his *katana*. He limped across the room, knelt down as far as his stiffened legs would allow, and picked it up. The blade was cool to the touch and badly bent, but it could be re-heated and re-forged.

Holding the damaged weapon, Tim trudged to the shattered main door of the foundry and stepped outside. Countless stars twinkled in the deep-blue, cloudless sky. In the distance, street lamps glowed over the darkened homes of countless sleeping families. It was Christmas Eve, and the city was safe. Tim turned and looked back for the last time into the deserted foundry, the final resting place of the Juggernauts. "They're dead," he observed aloud, his words echoing in the abyss. "Dead as coffin nails. It's ended."

About the Author

In addition to crafting great works of literature, Nicholas Kaminsky teaches college history as an adjunct instructor. Though he focused on American history while pursuing his M.A. degree, he somehow found himself teaching mostly about ancient and medieval Europe, which he's come to enjoy very much over the past several years. In his precious few moments of free time, he enjoys Batman, Star Wars, and bacon cheeseburgers.

www.nicholaskaminsky.com

www.ingramcontent.com/pod-product-compliance
Ingram Content Group UK Ltd.
Pitfield, Milton Keynes, MK11 3LW, UK
UKHW040022200726
13854UKWH00001B/305

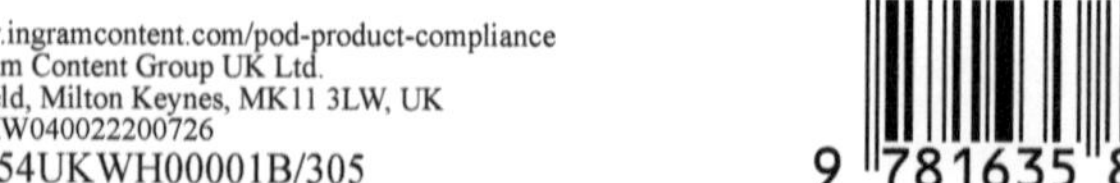

9 781635 871869